er tongue flicked and
d like that and she
en as her body sank
round Anthea's hips.
pulsing under her

couldn't restrain her
ea's heat and passion
. Her hands said stay

DO NOT WRITE ABOVE THIS LINE

JULIE A LANE

01707

5436843680010755
SAUGATUCK DOUGLAS HISTORICAL
SAUGATUCK MI
601101320600335E

SIGN HERE
X

The issuer of the card identified on this item is authorized to pay the amount shown as TOTAL (together with any other charges due thereon) subject to and in accordance with the agreement governing the use of such card. I promise to pay such TOTAL upon proper presentation.

EXPIRATION
DATE CHECKED

PLEASE DO NOT WRITE ABOVE THIS LINE

QTY. | CLASS | DESCRIPTION | PRICE | AMOUNT
1 | | Snapshots | 24 | 95
1 | | Item Two | 19 | 95

DATE 7/08/06
AUTHORIZATION 024846
REG./DEPT. CLERK

SUB TOTAL 44 90
TAX 2 69
TIP
MISC.

5703987
TOTAL 47 59

SALES SLIP
ORIGINAL

CAR POOL

Karin Kallmaker

Bella
BOOKS

2005

Bella Books, Inc.
P.O. Box 10543
Tallahassee, FL 32302

First published 1993 by Naiad Press

Printed in the United States of America on acid-free paper
First Edition

Editor: Christi Cassidy
Cover designer: Sandy Knowles

ISBN 1-59493-013-9

*For Maria, my Fortune
and
Joan McCarthy and Paula Lewis,
Newarkians of Note
and
the energetic, generous women of BACW*

The Fourth is for Freedom

About the Author

Karin's first crush on a woman was the local librarian. Just remembering the pencil through the loose, attractive bun makes her warm. Maybe it was the librarian's influence, but for whatever reason, at the age of 16 Karin fell into the arms of her first and only sweetheart.

There's a certain symmetry to the fact that ten years later, after seeing the film *Desert Hearts*, her sweetheart descended on the Berkeley Public Library to find some of "those" books. The books found there were the encouragement Karin needed to forget the so-called "mainstream" and spin her first romance for lesbians. That manuscript became her first novel, *In Every Port*.

The happily-ever-after couple now lives in the San Francisco Bay area, and became Mom and Moogie to Kelson in 1995 and Eleanor in 1997. They celebrate their twenty-eighth anniversary in 2005.

All of Karin's work can now be found at Bella Books. Details and background about her novels, and her other pen name, Laura Adams, can be found at www.kallmaker.com.

1
Road Block

"How many?" Anthea leaned back in the chair and schooled her expression to calm resignation.

"I have to drop five FTEs in the department by the end of the month." Her boss pushed his coffee cup away with a disconsolate expression.

"From which groups?" Anthea braced herself for the worst. To divert her anger, she turned on her mental video screen and the regional vice president became a paper doll dwarfed by an enormous pair of scissors. *Scissors beats paper.*

"Planning's going to have to drop three. You and reporting will make up the other two."

Just one person to cut . . . from a group of four responsible for refinery-wide product costing. Anthea gave herself a moment to snip the region veep's head off — *now that's what I call cutting waste* — then realized she had to decide who was going to go. There was no decision to be made, at least as far as she was concerned. "You know I've been wanting to get rid of Reed for the last two years."

Martin's expression hardened. "And nothing's changed. You're stuck with him."

"He's doing one-tenth the work Ruben is cranking out."

"Last hired, first fired. You know the policy as well as I do."

"But that means living with hiring mistakes forever. Not to mention the difference in salaries." Even to her ears, her usual argument sounded tired. More and more of her brain devoted itself to the spectacle of the gleaming scissors cutting a square out of Martin's likeness where the heart would be. Realizing her attention was wandering, she dismissed the mental video and mustered her arguments, even though she knew it was a lost battle. Cut one person this quarter, add two next quarter, cut two the quarter after that . . . it was an endless cycle which made no sense at all.

"I don't have to cut salaries, only bodies. Look, Reed is going to retire in another couple years —"

"Meanwhile, Ruben goes back on unemployment.

He's a damned hard worker. He's fast and accurate and intuitive. Cripes, Martin, the holidays are right around the corner and Ruben's got three kids." Anthea wasn't about to let him go without using every card she had. "And he's a person of color. NOC-U is supposed to be hiring and promoting people of color, *comprendo?*"

Martin frowned and looked nervous. Anthea hoped he was thinking about how much money and time an EEO action would cost. He cleared his throat. "Well, there's two spots available in product accounting —"

"Why not transfer Reed to one of them? I came up through product accounting. Let him retire on the job there."

Martin's lips tightened further. "Anthea, I'd love to do that. But Reed isn't going anywhere. You're just going to have to get used to that."

"So we lay off Ruben while Adrian and I get to do the work of four people." Because Reed wouldn't take on another single iota of work, Anthea thought. The old fart must have polished a lot of backside to be retired on the job. She and Martin had discussed Reed several times before. *When am I going to accept that I won't win?*

"It'll only be temporary," Martin said placatingly. "In another quarter the numbers will look better and we'll be able to hire back."

"Yeah, but with the recommendation I'm going to give him, Ruben will be working somewhere else by then. And I'll get to start over training someone which puts me behind even more. Martin, this just isn't fair to anybody."

3

"I'll try to get him hired on in product accounting," Martin said halfheartedly. "That's the breaks, kid. Nobody ever said business was fair."

Anthea would have said more, but a sense of overwhelming defeat closed her mouth and sent her stomping back to her cubicle. She threw herself into her chair, knocking her knee into the edge of her workstation. She swore softly but expressively and heard a sympathetic cluck from Adrian.

"Knee or elbow?" His voice carried easily over the cubicle barrier that divided their work areas.

"Knee. And I hate this job and this place and everything in it."

She heard Adrian get up and watched him appear from around the barrier between their two cubes. His nose appeared first, then a mass of unruly red hair, followed by large steel-rimmed glasses and finally his stick-pretzel body. Anthea had long decided he looked like a Yiddish Ichabod Crane. He sidled around the cubicle corner and sat down in her guest chair. "Does that include me?"

"If it weren't for you, I'd have blown this place a long time ago. Don't look so skeptical. I would have."

Adrian gave her a who-do-you-think-you're-fooling look. "It's me, remember? Quit? You? After what, ten years now? They know you won't."

"I could quit if I wanted to." Anthea sat up in indignation as Adrian's expression of disbelief didn't alter. "Just because I stick with things when the going gets rough doesn't mean I don't know when to bail out."

Adrian looked pointedly at the demure promise

ring Anthea wore — the one she'd exchanged with Lois on their first anniversary. "Right. You love change." His gaze transferred to her light gray blouse and deep teal-green suit. "If it hadn't been for the fire, you'd still be wearing navy blue, day in and day out."

Even though she resented his bluntness, Anthea knew Adrian was right. She had worn the office NOCCU uniform for several years until the Oakland firestorm had forced her to buy a new wardrobe. That winter navy blue had been out and other colors had invaded her business wear. "It's what they have in my size. If I were a seven instead of a twelve I could have my choice of colors."

Adrian made a mild sound of disgust. "If you were a seven you'd look like hell. One of these days you'll have to work to look decent, like the rest of us." He wearily passed his hand over his hair that ringed his head like Art Garfunkel's at its most global. "Everything looks good on you by pure accident. It's not as if you try."

"I do so try," Anthea said. "I bathe regularly." She added a superior sniff for emphasis.

"You're digressing . . . why do you hate this place more today than you did yesterday?"

Anthea sighed and pushed at the papers on her desk. "The S.O.B.s have won another round." She noticed Adrian looking at something down the cubicle-created hallway in puzzlement.

"What's Martin want with Ruben?"

"Ruben's on his way to Deep Space Nine." Her voice caught.

Adrian swiveled back toward her, staring at her for a minute, then said, "And the great straight white hope is keeping his job?"

"I'm told that's the breaks in business. Benefits of seniority."

"We could work here all our lives and not have the job security he has." Adrian took off his glasses to rub his eyes. "Damn. Ruben was just getting really productive. Want to go get drunk?" He put his glasses back on, then tried to smile, but his heart didn't appear to be in it.

"Not my style," Anthea said shortly. She wanted to go outside for a cigarette, but she had a transfer pricing mess to work out before the hysterical product managers called her again. From the quantity of voice mail they left for her they evidently thought Anthea was their personal business consultant. She sighed and turned toward her computer.

Adrian exhaled heavily, then went back to his cubicle.

"Did you guys get the usual end-of-quarter surprise?" Anthea shoved her briefcase onto the back seat and wiggled in after it. A needle of icy wind speared between her knees. There were no trees or buildings to cut the impact of the sharp December wind slicing its way from the southern San Francisco Bay and across the refinery parking lot. Lois was already buckled up. Anthea pulled her legs in and rubbed her arms to warm up. Celia settled herself into the passenger seat.

Lois answered after she had backed the car out. "Three people, but not me or Celia." She eased her foot on the gas pedal and Anthea took a moment to admire her lover's slender ankle, attached to a shapely calf.

"Well," Celia said. "I'm seriously thinking of looking for another job. I'm sick of this company and being treated like a yo-yo."

Lois did a double-take. "Cee-Cee, you must be kidding."

Celia patted Lois's hand on the gear shift. "I'll still keep up the tae kwon do class," she said.

Lois seemed about to say something, then didn't. Instead she stared fixedly ahead.

An awkward silence started to fill the car, so Anthea said, "It won't be easy to replace you in the car pool, but you should do what's best for you." She broke off, surprised by a furious glare from Lois. Did Lois really like Celia that much? She liked Celia, too. It had been really terrific when Celia, married with a little boy turning six, had joined their car pool, replacing an intense older man who did nothing unless Jesus personally told him it was okay. Within a few weeks Celia had figured out the relationship between Lois and Anthea and said she didn't mind. It would be hard to replace her, and Anthea would hate going back to pretending she and Lois didn't live together . . . telling little lies about Lois's imaginary apartment.

"Lois," Celia said in a pleading voice. "I'd have

talked to you about it sooner, but I didn't have a chance."

"Right. "

"Nothing has to change. . . ." Celia's voice trailed off and she turned to stare out the window.

Anthea looked from Celia to Lois, then glanced up into the rear view mirror, trying to catch a glimpse of Lois's face. What she saw shocked her . . . Lois's face was contorted with anger. After a minute ticked by, Lois said to Celia, "So you still want to continue the classes?"

Celia slowly turned back to Lois. Anthea decided later that if she hadn't been looking right at Celia she wouldn't have seen it — the quick dart of Celia's tongue as she licked her lips with an expression of . . . avarice. The same greed echoed hungrily in Lois's face.

Anthea digested the glance the two shared and shivered. *I'm wrong. Don't jump to conclusions.*

Except that Anthea had forgiven Lois one affair already. That was why Adrian didn't believe Anthea knew when to bail out of a bad situation. But the situation had been salvageable. It had been hard, but they had worked through it. Anthea had told herself things were even better after the trouble . . . they had talked so much it had seemed they were as close as they had ever been in their three years together. Even though the heat was finally reaching the back seat, she shivered again. The cold was coming from the pit of her stomach.

Closer . . . until about two months ago. Two months ago, management had threatened to close down Lois's entire department and transfer the functions to corporate headquarters in San Francisco.

8

The survival test had been a new product line campaign and Lois, along with others, had worked around the clock for nearly two weeks. Since then, that feeling of closeness hadn't come back. Lois had been exhausted. And then she had started those classes to help with stress . . . classes with Celia.

When they dropped Celia off, Celia said, "See you at class tonight?"

"Sure," Lois answered. Anthea couldn't tear her gaze away from the smile the two women shared.

"I'm sorry, Miss Sumoto, in spite of your work history and impeccable degree work, we can only offer you an entry-level position."

"Field geologist," Shay said weakly, then realized she was in danger of losing the only job offer she'd had in nearly two months of looking. "Well," she said in a brighter tone, "it's a start. I'm sure once I'm in the field I'll be able to demonstrate my practical experience."

"Yes, well, that will be up to your supervisors. At the end of probation, your salary will be reviewed along with an assessment of how your personal goals and the company goals mesh."

After wondering for a second how the goals of National Oil and Chemical Company U.S.A. could mesh with her own, Shay asked what her starting salary would be. Then she pretended the meagerness of it didn't shock her. She concluded the phone call as cheerily as possible, then crumpled into her only chair. She managed some rapid math in her head. She was trading intermittent temporary computer work — which paid better hourly, but wasn't full time — for a full-time job in her field.

The bottom line was that she would still have to work nights at the pizza parlor. She would have health insurance again. That was a plus even if she did have to wait three months for it, and she would be back in her field of work again, but as a low-paid well-digger. And a driving commute to pay for, all the way from Berkeley to the Palo Alto area. She could move closer, but where was she going to find a place she could have to herself for as little rent as she paid here?

Taking this job also meant working inside of the kind of corporation she and her father had so often been forced to oppose. Still, the job was within part of the company's environmental cleanup effort, and she could hope that people there were more in tune with the overall goal than corporate management representatives she'd worked with in the past. Even as she tried to tell herself everything would work out, she could imagine her father shaking his head at her in disappointment.

She forced herself to get up and go for a walk. If she sat in her tiny shoebox of a studio and looked at her chair, her bed and clock radio — the bulk of her personal assets, aside from the books — she would start to cry. Again.

If only, if only. If only Dad had gotten life insurance, she thought. If only the health insurance had covered more than sixty percent of the final cost of hospitalization and tests and doctors' reviews. One doctor alone, who had looked at her father for five minutes once a week, had charged almost five thousand dollars over the four months of intensive care. The insurance company said he had charged more than the market and of course, the doctor did not agree. Among the documents she had signed after the doctors told her her father was terminal was a promise to pay what insurance didn't cover. She'd agreed to all "medically necessary" treatment — good God, could she have done anything else? How could she have possibly put a price limit on keeping her father alive?

After the funeral, she had sold everything possible to pay down the hospital and funeral bills. Even their laptop, which she deeply regretted now. There hadn't been much to sell and she was still neck-deep in debt.

Sumoto & Sumoto had traveled light and fast. The Exxon *Valdez*, Gulf War, military base closures, hurricanes and everyday industrial toxic waste cleanups had kept them busy and, literally, all over the globe. If her father had known how short his time was, and how hard his illness would hit Shay, he would have planned differently, she was certain. He wouldn't have worked the last two jobs for expenses only, even if it was for money-poor nonprofits. If only he hadn't smoked three packs a day and if only he had gone to a doctor before he'd started coughing up pieces of his lungs. If only Shay hadn't been so self-absorbed in her first assignment as team leader in the predevelopment of a groundwater cleanup site. She might have forced him to a doctor sooner — if only, if only, and he might still be alive.

She had hoped being Glen Sumoto's daughter would at least get her interviews, but it hadn't worked out that way. How did you put on a resume that you'd been devil's advocate and sounding board to one of the most brilliant minds in environmental engineering? Everyone had apparently failed to notice that Shay had been her father's partner — not his secretary. And now she was going to dig wells on an oil refinery.

She kicked a rock out of her path, then stopped to watch the dogs in the Ohlone Dog Park. Three Labrador puppies rolled like gymnasts in a tussling tug of war over a small stick. Leave it to Berkeley to have a park for dogs, she thought. The only compensation for her tiny apartment, which she guessed had once been a garage under the main living quarters, was its situation right across Hearst from the park.

Well, there were two compensations. The second was Mrs. Giordano, who lived upstairs from Shay and had decided Shay needed mothering. Mothering included supper on Sundays if Shay didn't have plans, which Shay never did. It wasn't as if she ever had a moment to make other friends. Making friends took a lot of energy and she didn't have any to spare.

She felt attached to the Bay Area for some reason she couldn't fathom. She had no friends here, only a few friends worldwide, actually. Maybe she was hanging around because this was where her father had died and leaving meant he'd really gone, she thought. Tears welled up and she concentrated on watching the puppies for a few minutes. When she felt more at peace, she decided to drop in on Mrs. Giordano to tell her the good news. Such as it was.

Feeling better — thinking about Mrs. Giordano

always made Shay feel better — she walked back toward her apartment. She earned her supper on Sundays by helping Mrs. Giordano clean up after her unofficial Sunday "soup" kitchen. Mrs. Giordano didn't make soup; she made lasagna and pizza and spaghetti, all authentic Northern Italian cuisine, and better yet, nutritious, hot and plentiful. Anyone from the small senior citizens' apartment building down the street could drop in, have a meal and a chat and no money ever changed hands.

From the looks of some of the old people, Mrs. Giordano's Sunday meal was all that stood between them and pet food meatloaf. Shay was happy to help and it certainly gave her someone to feel sorry for besides herself. Now she would have a day-to-day grind and wouldn't be able to help out as much as she had during the week. At least she'd still be able to contribute ingredients from the pizza parlor whenever the owner felt generous.

She bounded up the steps, glad at least that she hadn't had an assignment for the day and was at home to take the call about the job.

"You've been out without your coat again," Mrs. Giordano observed. "You need some hot chocolate."

"It's very mild today, just overcast," Shay said in her defense, following Mrs. Giordano to her kitchen. "But hot chocolate sounds fabulous. I'm celebrating."

Mrs. Giordano faced Shay, one gnarled hand pressing against the gold cross she wore at her throat. "You have a steady job! I knew it would happen soon."

"You're a mind reader." Shay always thought Mrs. Giordano's hands looked like the roots of cypress trees. Hard and strong, her fingers dug down

13

into dough when Shay's tiny hands could no longer knead it, and when she was through the mound of flour and water would be as soft as a baby's tushy, on its way to becoming something unbelievably scrumptious — pizza dough, breadsticks or foccacio.

Mrs. Giordano bustled to make two cups of hot chocolate. She made it the old-fashioned way, with milk, baker's chocolate and sugar in a saucepan — nothing instant for Mrs. Giordano. "Well, now you'll have time to get out and have some friends your own age."

"Well, it's in my field of work, but the pay is lousy. I'll have to keep working at the pizza parlor. The rent isn't going to go down." Mrs. Giordano would only get upset if Shay told her she paid almost as much for her studio as Mrs. Giordano did for the two-bedroom apartment she'd lived in for twenty-three years. Rent control had certainly worked for her.

"That's a terrible thing. A crime," Mrs. Giordano said passionately. "You'll be exhausted every day. At least you could take off one or two nights each week. A good girl like you shouldn't have to work so hard."

"I'm young." Shay appreciated Mrs. Giordano's sympathy more than she could show — without crying — but she didn't want Mrs. Giordano to worry about her. "I have good bones." Mrs. Giordano put great faith in good bones.

The older woman laughed. "If you keep working in the pizza parlor, you're never going to meet a nice boy who will take all this worry off your shoulders."

"Mrs. Giordano," Shay said slowly, her voice

fading away. She took a deep breath. "It doesn't work that way anymore. It takes two people working hard to live as well as their parents did on one income. Chances are, anyone I might meet would be just as tight for cash as I am."

"You should have a chance to meet a nice fellow." Mrs. Giordano shook her head. She tested the heat of the chocolate with the tip of her thumb, then poured the hot mixture into mugs without a single spilled drop. "Someone to share your troubles. It makes a good marriage, sharing troubles the way I did with my Harry, may he rest in peace. Now drink up, there's more where that came from."

"Mrs. Giordano," Shay began. She really liked the old lady, but she had promised herself that as soon as Mrs. Giordano brought anything of this sort up, she would say her piece. Her heart rate tripled and she set her mug down to make her shaking hands less obvious. Saying what she had to say didn't get any easier with practice. "It would be nice to share my troubles with someone I loved. But it wouldn't be with a fellow. It would be with a woman."

Mrs. Giordano blinked at her, her mug of chocolate poised halfway to her mouth. "Are you one of those lesbians?" Her thinning eyebrows, carefully and tastefully penciled to a darker brown, disappeared under her elegantly coifed brunette wig.

"That's me," Shay said. She smiled, but anxiously searched Mrs. Giordano's expression for her true feelings.

"Goodness gracious. To think of the trouble I've been having to get materials for the old gay people at the center and I could have just asked you, don't you know. I called the Area Agency on Aging and you would have thought I'd asked for pornography. All I wanted was someone to speak at one of our meetings about groups that are available and such." Mrs. Giordano pursed her lips and shook her head sagely. "This state is being run into the ground," she pronounced. She set her mug down with an emphatic thunk.

Shay blinked rapidly and then stared into her hot chocolate to hide how close to tears she was. "There's a group called Gay and Lesbian Outreach to Elders. They'll be in the Yellow Pages under Gay and Lesbian Organizations."

Mrs. Giordano threw up her hands. "The phone book! Why didn't I think of the phone book?"

Shay tried her best to look nonchalant. "We're pretty respectable these days."

"My dear, you are a godsend. Have some more chocolate," Mrs. Giordano said. "Mrs. Stein and Mrs. Kroeger are going to be thrilled. I just don't see how the Lord would begrudge them comfort in their old age — they've only got each other, don't you know." She made a noise that was something between a snort and a cough. "But try telling Father Donohue that. I've given up." She patted Shay's hand.

"You have an unusual faith." Shay returned the pat. She sipped her chocolate and continued to fight tears. For the first time since her father's death she felt warm inside, in places all the hot chocolate in the world couldn't reach.

She changed the topic to Mrs. Giordano's favorite soap opera and sat down to watch it with her. She didn't follow the plot. Instead, she tried to work out her schedule. And how on earth was she going to get to work? She had to drive almost to San Jose. It had been a forty-five-minute drive during non-rush times for the interview. During rush hour ... she mentally added up the cost of bridge tolls and gas. She would definitely be working every night at the pizza parlor, and a long Saturday shift, too. She thought about how little sleep there would be.

She should probably look at the rest of this week and the next as a vacation, because there wouldn't be any rest for a long time. And her only diversion would be dreams about a woman, any woman, lots of women. Dreams were very unsatisfying but it looked as if that would be all she'd have for a while longer.

Anthea wasn't asleep when Lois came in from her class. She kept quiet, waiting until Lois had dozed off ... something Lois did quickly after class with Celia. When Anthea was sure Lois wouldn't be disturbed, she slowly slid out of bed.

God, I feel like something out of a Movie of the Week ... the jealous wife, searching through hubby's clothes. If she was wrong, she'd never be suspicious again, she told herself. Quietly, she picked up the clothes Lois had discarded. Somehow, her scruples had prevented her from searching through Lois's private files for credit card slips or other incriminating evidence. But her scruples had no problem with doing laundry. Even if it was nearly midnight.

She was briefly at war with herself. There was, she had decided, only one way to know for sure ... *I won't look.* But she did. It was nothing that a court of law would take as proof and most likely Lois would deny anything had happened. But Lois's panties had all the evidence Anthea needed. Tae kwon do did not elicit that kind of physical response. Only intense, prolonged arousal did that. A wave of nausea hit her as her mental video screen created a too-accurate vision of Celia's fingers sliding around the elastic to arouse Lois even further... Celia stroking what Anthea loved to touch... Lois making that choking cry when she came, but with Celia holding her afterward.

The collar of her shirt was damp... not with sweat, but water from damp hair. Lois had taken a shower. *And why did I believe classes would last until midnight?* Because you wanted to, she told herself.

She had been under deadlines at work. Lois had certainly had her share of stress in marketing. There had been days when all Anthea needed was a touch of her hand, a quiet kiss and the comfort of her arms. She had thought their need for each other had just taken a different form lately... something less passionate, but still very comforting. Clearly it wasn't enough for Lois. It looked as if Lois, after all the work on "building communication" they'd done after that first affair, hadn't wanted to talk to Anthea about it. She'd just gone elsewhere.

To a straight woman who was probably just having kicks.

Anthea twisted the incriminating panties into a ball. She felt despicable and cheap. She wanted to break something. She wanted to throw up. She wanted to pull Lois out of bed and scream at her. She wanted to wail and tear her hair.

Keep control. Control was the legacy of too many

years of living with alcoholic parents. Control was the legacy of rebuilding her life and home after the firestorm had taken everything away.

She wrapped herself in her robe and sat in the kitchen, comforting herself with a cigarette. She told herself she should decide what to do about Lois and this affair. She chose what to wear to work in the morning. She mentally drew up a list of the steps she should take to quit smoking. She thought about the time survey presentation she had to give first thing out in the field. She remembered how she had fallen in love with Lois. She had another cigarette.

"Safety meeting." Harold slapped Shay on the back and she jerked her head up. *Oh shit.* Second week on the job and she still didn't have a grip on the schedule. She'd forgotten about the Monday Morning Horror and now she wouldn't have time to get another cup of coffee. Scott noticed who came in late. She trailed after Harold and staggered into the tiny conference room.

The forty or so people on the Groundwater Protection Grip Project squished together for the weekly safety meeting, with at least a dozen standing around the perimeter. This week's discussion was on what to do in the case of a hydrogen-sulfide gas leak. Right, Shay thought. I'll cover my mouth and nose with something and be dead in eight seconds instead of five, like everyone else. The discussion was brief, which Shay took as a sign that everyone understood that a leak of that nature was deadly and protecting yourself was futile.

She started to get up but the head of the project cleared his throat and stood up. Shay stifled a yawn and settled onto the hard seat again.

After a couple of sentences about management policy, leaving Shay sleepier than ever — would she ever be awake in the morning again, she wondered — he jabbed a thumb in the direction of a woman sitting behind him.

The woman stood up . . . damn, she'd missed her name. Shay guessed her blue-green suit had cost the price of a month's rent and then some. She noticed cynically that the woman held herself away from everything around her, as if she were afraid that the inevitable grime of a working field trailer would rub off on her pristine clothes or muss the French braid of her gold-reddish hair.

" —so don't shoot the messenger," the woman was saying. She smiled with a certain amount of charm, Shay admitted grudgingly. "What I'm passing out are time survey sheets. For a period of four weeks starting today, you'll need to keep track of everything you do in twenty-minute increments."

Shay, along with almost everyone else, groaned loudly. French Braid smiled again. "I'm sorry, but there's no way around it. And you should be thankful . . . not too many years ago, efficiency specialists insisted that constant, endless record-keeping was the only accurate way to measure performance and calculate costs. A time survey like this one is still accurate at a much lower expense to the company. And of course it's much easier on you."

"What do you mean by 'performance'?" The project head, who had been espousing the management line, suddenly looked concerned.

French Braid's charming smile didn't fade. Shay thought her smile was too rehearsed. Obviously, she'd answered the question a hundred times. "Performance in a costing sense is not the same thing as performance in our annual reviews. To us in product costing, performance is the completion of a task — we don't have a good or bad judgment to place on anything. Our sole concern is what tasks were completed, how long they took, and what product they contributed to."

"But we're environmental cleanup, not a product," someone said.

"Groundwater Protection Grid, I know. You're an overhead item. But your costs have to be transferred to products. In a way, your unit is like legal, or marketing, or like my unit, product costing." Again, the perfect lips curved in a charming smile. Shay got the picture now. Their unit was going to be added up, a cost assigned and then management would start screaming at the regulators about how much was being spent to comply with their petty directives, like finding out why the xylene toxicity level was increasing in one of the testing wells.

Sure, this project wasn't cheap, but there was a ton of dead weight that could be cut — at least that's how she saw it after a quick review of the organizational chart. Shay heard herself ask, "Why now?"

French Braid shrugged slightly. "Good a time as any. I understand you're fully staffed and you're just beginning the first major phase of this project. We survey the whole refinery over a course of two years. You came up in the rotation."

Maybe it was the lack of coffee, but Shay found

herself really disliking this woman. She was so . . . poised. A consummate professional. Shay glanced down at her wrinkled jeans and no-brand tennis shoes, consciously setting aside a feeling of dowdiness. She was too tired to make an effort with her clothes, even if she thought it was important, which she didn't. Fancy clothes were only required if visiting the Exec Building, a place Shay had no intention of going. And she didn't believe the timing was random . . . they had just reached full staffing and now management wanted numbers to wave at the Water Quality Board. She'd been in plenty of meetings where it had happened. This woman was an accessory before the fact.

She took her time sheet — the NOCCU logo neatly imprinted at the top in blue as it was on every piece of paper in the place — and attempted to look interested as French Braid explained how to fill it in. They practiced by filling in the time already spent this morning at the safety meeting. She was disliking working for a large corporation even more than she had thought she would.

When the meeting was over she filled up her mug and wandered back toward the cubicle she shared with Harold. She had a mountain of data to enter and she should look sharp about it.

"Hey, Sumoto." She jerked her head in the direction of her immediate supervisor's voice. Scott beckoned her to join him and French Braid.

"Andy needs a lift back to the Exec Building. Could you take her over? Just pick up a car key from the office." Scott walked away without waiting for Shay's response.

"Let me put my coffee down and get a vehicle key," Shay said.

"I'll be right here," Andy said, with another of those charming, brittle smiles. Shay decided Andy really hated being in the field . . . tension was written all over her and her eyes, now that Shay was close enough to see that they were gray, were rimmed in red. Andy — what could that possibly be short for? Andrea maybe. Andy's only detectable makeup had been applied to camouflage heavy circles — twins to the ones under Shay's own eyes. Shay didn't bother to cover them. She didn't have time to spend on makeup, though it looked as if French Braid spent hours every morning. Her complexion was so flawless it had to come out of a bottle. A very expensive bottle.

Without analyzing why, Shay chose the key to the oldest of the field trucks. Andy followed her to the parking lot and waited as Shay made a show of spreading a clean towel over the less than clean bench seat. Andy perched on the towel, but didn't say anything or suggest taking one of the cars that also sat in the parking lot. In the enclosed space, Shay could immediately tell that Andy smoked. After watching her father die, the smell of cigarettes turned her stomach.

Neither of them said anything during the brief ride to the Exec Building. Shay rolled down the window to let in cold, but fresh air. The faint smell of chemicals and gasoline was preferable to cigarettes. Shay made a great show of obeying the refinery driving laws . . . five miles an hour, complete stops at all signs. They wound through the overhead piping, flare points and container tracks, at one point stopping for another truck, filled to the top with dirt from a site. A group of workers — all Hispanic, as far as Shay could tell — leaned on shovels next to a wide, shallow excavation while their supervisor, a white male and the only person wearing a hard hat, spoke into a field phone. What on earth were they digging up, she wondered. From the color of the soil, she would have thought the lot of them should be wearing filter masks.

When their path was clear again, Shay turned into the only landscaped area on the refinery. Andy slid out of the truck as Shay pulled up at the Exec Building North entrance.

"Thanks for the lift," Andy said, her smile completely faded. Shay gave her a mocking salute and pulled away as soon as Andy closed the door. She had a lot of data to enter and now, thanks to French Braid, a time survey to fill out.

Anthea barely made it through the rest of her day. When she called Lois to suggest having lunch together, Lois had said she was too busy . . . for the fourth time in a row. For two weeks she had been trying to make extra efforts — romantic dinners prepared that Lois said she was too tired to eat. She'd made physical overtures, only to find Lois beset with a series of ailments . . . headache, indigestion, backache. If it hadn't been happening to her, Anthea would have advised herself to read the handwriting on the wall. She didn't want to let three years go so easily. Not that Lois showed any signs of wanting to go. *She likes it just the way it is — sex on the outside and me to turn on the electric blanket at night.*

Anthea knew her self-esteem was in the basement. She'd let that technician shove her into a filthy truck, for God's sake, and treat her like a piece of furniture. She hadn't cared enough at the time to suggest using one of the cars and now, every time she spotted the grimy stain on the side of her skirt, it made her angry. She was tired of letting people walk all over her. Adrian didn't believe she could take control of her life. Because it's true, she thought.

It didn't help that it was Ruben's last day. He said he understood the trap Anthea was in, but she could feel the hurt and sense of injustice from him. Especially when Reed had just refused to take over any of Ruben's work, which was typical, but he had plenty of time to handle the United Way drive and organize the floor's Christmas party. She had tried to work with Reed, but he just went to Martin and the two of them had a good ol' chat and then Martin told her that Reed seemed to have plenty of work. It made Anthea want to scream.

She did the only thing she could under her discretion — she gave Ruben the small performance bonus she could authorize on her own. She also had the Christmas bonus coupons ready to hand out to her staff. Since Ruben's last day fell before the day she was supposed to hand them out, she hadn't been given a set for him. Silently cursing NOC-U's cheapness — lots of paper doll heads were rolling — she gave him the set she'd been given for herself. At least his kids would have a tree to decorate and they could get a ten-pound ham for free. She also pretended that the coupon book normally included a hundred-dollar gift certificate at the local grocery store. It wasn't much in the way of blood money, but Ruben was proud and smart . . . he wouldn't believe it was coming from the company if she tried to give him more.

She felt as if she were standing at the bottom of the mountain watching an avalanche made up of all the failures of her life head straight for her. It got bigger when she said goodbye to Ruben. It gathered speed as she watched Lois and Celia interact during the ride home.

Eight times Celia managed to find excuses to touch Lois . . . there, that was nine. *Can't she think of something more subtle than "there's a piece of lint on your shoulder"?* Who did they think they are fooling, she stormed to herself. Me, obviously. Anthea tried to impel herself to act. To do something. She'd tried to connect with Lois in subtle ways, and they weren't working.

She closed her eyes against her anger and abruptly fell asleep, another restless night of cigarettes catching up all at once. Anthea was disoriented when she got out of Celia's car, and didn't join Lois's wave as Celia drove away. She had crossed the kitchen by the time Lois was closing the front door. The futility of pretending nothing was wrong washed over her. She didn't turn to face Lois as she said, "Why are you sleeping with Celia?"

Lois didn't say anything and Anthea slowly turned to face her. Irrelevant thoughts occurred to her . . . the kitchen floor needed washing. She looked at Lois and met an expression of defiance.

26

"It was better than nothing," Lois finally said, all in a rush, from across the kitchen. "When you finally do want to have sex . . . it's like having sex with a computer. Boring."

She didn't even bother to deny it, not like last time. Anthea widened her eyes to hide a shimmer of tears. She wasn't going to let Lois hurt her. She wasn't going to wimp out this time and forgive her. "You don't think she's going to leave her husband and child for you, do you? You can't be that stupid."

Lois's fingers clenched around the keys she still held. "You might be surprised. Celia is in love with me."

Anthea allowed herself an unbelieving laugh. "I suppose she told you this during that class you both have been taking for the last three months."

Lois's lips curved in a vicious smile as she crossed her arms over her chest. "What class?"

Anthea thought, I'm not hurt yet, I can head it off. "Why couldn't you just tell me you didn't love me anymore? Why let me find out like this?"

"Who said I didn't love you anymore?"

I haven't heard you say you do! "You have a funny way of showing it. A very painful way of showing it."

"I still have feelings for you — "

"So it seems," Anthea said. "Like *boredom.* I don't think that's the kind of feeling that makes for a good relationship. And lying to me about a class so you can have an affair, that doesn't help things either."

"What do you expect from me? We're suffering from lesbian bed death."

Anthea steadied herself with a deep breath. "You

27

don't seem to have any problems being sexual. You just don't want to be sexual with me. So call it what you like. Give it a clinical name. I'm sure somewhere you've found some self-help book that says having an affair is the best way to cure it."

"I'm supposed to go without sex?"

"You promised you'd talk to me if you felt this way."

"If I told you I was having an affair, you'd go off the deep end like last time."

The deep end? In Anthea's opinion, she'd behaved in a very civilized manner last time. Couples counseling, long talks, a romantic vacation. "You promised," she said again, her voice failing her. She was going to cry. Her throat seized up and it hurt to breathe. *I won't let her make me cry.*

Lois stared sullenly across the kitchen at her. Anthea met her gaze as steadily as she could manage. She fought down the tears and found some inner core of strength. "Well, that's that. Since you were so sure I'd go off the deep end, I guess I will. This is my house, so I think you'd better start packing."

Lois dropped her jaw. "You don't think I'm going to move out at a moment's notice, do you? It will be impossible to find an apartment in Berkeley."

Anthea straightened her shoulders. "You should have thought of that before you started screwing around with Celia. What did you think I'd do, invite you two to use the guest room? I'd like you out of here now, if not sooner."

Lois made a sound of disbelief. "I think you have a lot of possessiveness issues. You're just trying to hurt me by throwing me out."

Damn right, Anthea thought. *Of course I'm trying to hurt you! I can't believe you did what you did — you promised it wouldn't happen again.* Anthea clamped down on her anger. "Are you implying it would be good for my psyche not to end our relationship? I should let you go on sleeping around?"

"I think you're just acting out some old issues with your parents —"

"Don't you dare," Anthea said in a voice that came painfully out of her chest. "Don't you dare imply that if I had worked out my feelings about my parents I wouldn't care about you cheating on me. Sure I have possessiveness issues, I happen to feel possessiveness is just fine in moderation. I think it's pretty moderate to want honesty and fidelity from someone I love."

Lois drew herself up with a grimace of distaste. "The least you can do —"

"Is not let you walk all over me again. You break our agreement and expect me to show you consideration? To be kind and forgiving? Once was enough for me."

Lois shook her head slowly. "Is that all it was, an agreement?" Her voice rose. "A relationship isn't something you can notarize. Don't you want to talk about it? That's all you ever want to do."

"I've been trying to talk to you for two weeks, but you're just not there. So I have nothing to say," Anthea said, forcing her voice to steely calm. "You, on the other hand, had plenty to tell me. But you didn't say a word. You've forgone your right to ask for my consideration."

"You have got to be the most wooden person I

have ever met!" Lois's voice peaked at a shrill. "Can't you show some emotion for once?"

"Is that why you did it? To make me feel something? That's . . . sick."

"You said you forgave me that nothing little fling, but you've been about as warm as a glacier ever since. You don't have a spontaneous bone left in your body. Not that you were ever open to being spontaneous."

"Is 'spontaneous' a new euphemism for thinking with your crotch? I'm not spontaneous because I'm not sleeping around?" Anthea bit her lower lip to steady her voice. "Is spontaneous what you are? Do I call you that instead of deceitful?"

"Even when you're pissed off, you're anal retentive. You don't even care enough about me to get mad," Lois said. "You don't have a real emotion in your entire body."

Anal retentive — well, she'd let that go by. Her voice was even and low as she said, "Would you feel better if I yelled and threw things? You used to think my . . . even temper was a good point."

"It doesn't outweigh your negatives. So you have a nice house but the silence in here is deafening."

"And you liked the vacations, didn't you? And the season tickets to Berkeley Rep and the Women's Philharmonic and the San Francisco Ballet and —"

"And that's another thing. I'm tired of the crushing obligation I feel just because you pay for all the luxuries. I never forget it." Lois exhaled loudly. "I'm still in the doghouse about that lousy vase."

"I never said anything —"

"I know, but the place where it was is still

empty. It's like you're reproaching me every second of every day."

"It wasn't special —"

"But it was yours. Everything in here is yours."

"When did you start hating that that's the way it was?" Anthea was truly bewildered now. What had Lois expected from her — community property without any commitment? Anthea had hinted that she would like to register as domestic partners, but Lois had shrugged it off.

Lois was shaking her head. "Oh, I don't know. You're stifling me. You can't blame me for looking for fun somewhere else."

"Oh, I see. This is my fault," Anthea said with a mocking smile. "I'm not the one having an affair with the other woman in our car pool. So okay, don't call me adventurous."

"I won't call you a lesbian either. The closet you live in is so tight I can't breathe. I've had enough of it." Lois stalked out of the kitchen, the crack of her heels echoing irately over the tile.

It's not fair, Anthea thought. *She acts like I forced her to sleep with Celia.* She realized she was still holding her briefcase. She set it down in its accustomed place next to the living room door. She wasn't going to follow Lois to fight. It wasn't worth it. She needed to think.

She stepped out onto the deck. Following the redwood railing, she walked to the end farthest from the house where the wind was the strongest. Loose tendrils of hair at her temples whipped back from her eyes. From here she could see the flickering lights of Marin, fifteen miles or more — two bridges and a big bay away. Yesterday's rain had left the air clear and sharp, and it had brought the temperature up to a mellow mid-sixty range. At her feet, seemingly close enough to touch, she watched someone's headlights illuminating the incline behind the Claremont Hotel on their way up to this neighborhood. She wished she had brought a cigarette outside with her, but right now she wouldn't go back inside to get one.

She watched the Oakland *Tribune* building's red neon lights flicker on and off until she was shivering. She thought she was cold, but when she went inside the shivering didn't stop. She was shivering with anger. Control, she told herself. *If you lose control there's no telling what you might do. Don't risk it.*

Lois was in jeans and a T-shirt . . . the black T-shirt that made Anthea want to slide her hands under it, up, unhook Lois's bra. . . . Anthea shook the image out of her mind. Lois didn't want her anymore. She stomped from the garage to the bedroom again, and Anthea kept out of her way. Her hands itched for something to do, but she wasn't going to offer to help, so she made a salad and forced herself to eat it. She forced herself to do the dishes. She forced herself not to watch as Lois carried yet another box out to her car.

Well, this departure would be quick. Having lost everything in the fire that had swept across the East Bay hills, Lois had been renting all her furniture when Anthea met her. Since they had moved in together a few months later, Lois had never replaced what she lost. She had preferred spending her money on clothes and her annual solo vacation . . . and tae kwon do classes.

Why had she forgiven Lois that first affair? Was forgiving it permission to do it again?

Lois appeared with a paper bag from the top of which peeked the hair dryer and a bra. I guess I'll be using the travel dryer, Anthea thought. Lois paused for a moment, the door to the garage open, and Anthea looked up from the sink.

"Monica is putting me up until I find a place."

That figures, Anthea thought. Monica had been the first affair.

"Well," Lois said, "I wish you the best of commuting by yourself. I'm guessing you won't want to ride with us. I'm sure you'll find some new people for a pool."

"The car pool pass is in my name. It's been in my name for six years."

"Don't be childish. It's two against one. It should be ours."

"Possession is nine-tenths." The car outside was locked and the alarm system was on. Anthea swept a crumb from the counter into the sink. She dusted her hands. *I'll be damned if I'll give it to them.* All she needed was to find one more person and she'd be back in car pool business again . . . it only took two to use car pool lanes on this side of the bay and to get a parking pass at the refinery.

Lois swept out of the kitchen, yanking the door closed after her.

The vibration from the slamming door knocked a

porcelain sconce off its hook. Anthea jabbed her thumb on a sharp edge as she cleaned up the shattered pieces.

She wished she had said, just for the record, that Lois wasn't leaving her, she was throwing Lois out. It seemed an important distinction. She dabbed a little peroxide on the cut, then carefully wound a Band-Aid over it.

There. Now everything would be okay. Her thumb throbbed for a while, then it went numb. She wondered when she would start missing Lois. She smoked one cigarette after another in between spoonfuls of a pint of Ben & Jerry's New York Super Fudge Chunk, telling herself all the while what she was really upset about was having to commute alone.

She would not cry. She hadn't cried since she was seven and she wouldn't start now.

2

Compression Check

Anthea stomped on the gas pedal. The Legend surged forward, covering the unexpected two-car length gap ahead of her in moments. She slammed on the brakes and stopped a few inches short of tapping bumpers. "Only another fifteen minutes to the bridge at this rate," she said aloud, glaring in the rear view mirror. Behind her — and ahead as well — was the usual massive line-up to get on the frontage that bypassed some of the freeway leading to the Dumbarton Bridge. It was slightly faster than taking the freeway all the way. Even though there was no toll this direction, it still took longer to get on the bridge going home than on the way to work.

She fumbled in her purse on the passenger seat for a cigarette, then remembered her New Year's resolution. No smoking in the car. One after breakfast. One from car to the office. One at each of her two self-allotted breaks, maybe one at lunch. One when she got home and then after dinner whatever was left of her half-pack allocation. She could hear Lois telling her she was being anal retentive about quitting.

"Shut the fuck up, Lois," Anthea said to her reflection in the mirror. One of the many consequences of commuting alone was the habit she was developing of talking to herself and the dreadful language she was getting too accustomed to using. She reached the turn to the frontage road and quickly pulled out. The Legend settled down to a steady pace of twenty miles per hour.

She'd spent her afternoon going over the time survey data from the Groundwater Protection unit — something Ruben would have done if he'd still been there. The task had recalled the way she'd let that . . . that . . . *technician* treat her. She had only been doing her job — there was no reason to be treated like a leper. It was bad enough her unit didn't get any respect from upper management. It was bad enough that Lois had treated her like a doormat. But to let some complete stranger step all over her self-esteem like that . . . what had she been trying to prove, that Anthea wasn't up to the rigors of field work?

36

She'd been through every inch of that refinery at one time or another, back in her product accounting days, explaining time surveys, or learning the manufacturing stages, and she'd done it in heels and a suit when her tour guides and hosts had worn boots and jeans. She probably knew more about production than everyone in Groundwater combined. Accountants had to know everything about everything or they couldn't do their job. Something Ms. Superior Field Geologist obviously didn't think about. Something Lois had never believed. Accounting, she had said, was an exact and limited science. No creativity. Not like marketing, where it was tense, tense, tense every minute keeping up with competition. Marketing was an art form.

Hah.

Anthea turned the cassette player volume up, but it was already too late. She was thinking about Lois again. The BMW in the next lane began to merge over into Anthea's door. She honked, swore, yelled, honked again, and when the car veered off, she gave the driver the finger. She saw the older man's eyes widen in panic, as if he thought Anthea was going to pull a shotgun out and squeeze off a couple of rounds in retribution. *I'm turning into the kind of driver I hate.*

Traffic came to a complete halt, then sluggishly moved forward again. Anthea leaned on her horn when the driver ahead didn't fill up the gap in front of him, allowing three cars from the adjacent lane to merge ahead. Her car inched forward. Her pressure must be off the scale, she thought — partly the traffic, and partly because she was thinking about what Lois had said about her being a computer.

37

When Anthea had met her briefly to hand over some more clothing she'd come across, Lois had reiterated that fact, and added a few more along the same lines, accusing Anthea of being unsupportive during Lois's transition and summing her up as heartless and selfish. *How was I supposed to be supportive...help her move? Pay the deposit on her apartment? And heartless is calling up CPS and saying the car pool was dissolved so I had to turn in the pass and park in the hinterlands again.*

The bitch.

Maybe, Anthea thought, Lois was trying to deliberately provoke her. Make Anthea take her back again, like last time. But there was no going back. Okay, she acknowledged that ever since the first affair, she'd held a piece of herself aloof. She didn't want to get hurt again. She didn't want to trust again. So maybe Lois was justified in saying Anthea had cooled a little.

She hit the horn again for the fifth time in as many minutes and realized she had become a raving shrew. Still, she had to yell at someone. It was therapeutic. Adrian had expressed his opinion — in terms so plain as to avoid any misunderstanding — that she had been a virago lately. They both felt completely overworked and abused, and because she was the boss Adrian got to blame her, which made her feel worse. She blamed her boss, but Martin hardly cared, so blaming him lacked any psychic value. She missed Ruben's competence. She would cheerfully kick Reed's butt out the nearest window.

Martin had asked one day if there was something wrong, but what was she supposed to say? That she wanted Ruben back? It would have only pissed him off. That she was going through a divorce? She didn't have the right to say that. God knew she'd listened to him during his divorce. But because she'd never been — and couldn't be — legally married, she wasn't allowed the same sympathy in return. Somehow it wasn't supposed to be as big a deal if they'd never been married. There were no legal formalities to go through. But the house was just as empty, the rejection was just as painful, she hurt all day every day and it wasn't getting better like she thought it would. And because she'd been the one to insist on ending it, what friends she and Lois had had in common blamed her for the breakup.

When she reached the ramp to the freeway, she seized an opening to cross several lanes and position herself for the fast lane. After a mile or so, the pace abruptly increased, and Anthea floored the accelerator for the steep ascent. As she picked up speed, Anthea found she was able to let go of the memories again. As soon as the traffic backed up, she felt trapped. When she felt trapped, she thought about Lois. When she thought about Lois she went over the same stretch of road again and again.

She told herself to start thinking positively. Maybe she was entering a lucky period. Lord knew she was due. Maybe this week she would find out that someone else who worked at the refinery wanted to car pool from the East Bay.

And maybe today was the last time she'd think about Lois. The bitch.

Shay yanked her heel out of the grate and swore.

It was a choice phrase she'd picked up from a wildcatter. There was no one around, which was fortunate. Tottering on one leg, she examined her damaged shoe.

The leather on the back of the pump had been scraped up the heel. The cover had come off completely, leaving the bare nail exposed. They were the last dress shoes — *had been* the last pair — she owned that were wearable. She couldn't afford a cobbler, much less a new pair, much less the time to take shoes to a repair shop anyway. It did not improve her humor at all that she usually wouldn't be caught dead in heels.

What had possessed her to take this job? Why hadn't she just moved out of the area? She must have been in shock to have agreed. Why hadn't she followed up periodically with the people she knew at EPA — like Joan Lewis? Joan would have helped her. Why hadn't she sent her resume to the big environmental engineering firms? Even though EPA was on everyone's unpopular list, it was better than private industry. So the engineering firms were completely male dominated and mostly in cahoots with the corporations — conditions slightly better than this hell hole. And this hell hole was a corporation. She put her shoe back on and stomped on across the asphalt of the vast parking lot. With every step she added another word to the litany that began, "Patriarchal, fascist, sexist. . . ."

As she reached the other side and went through the double doors into the hallway she winced at the loud click her bare heel made on the echoing floor. She sounded like a one-legged tap dancer. And she blamed the car pool services department and good ol'

NOC-U. It had only taken three months for her to feel an incredible level of contempt for it — she felt like Living Dead.

She could have used inter-refinery mail to forward the paperwork to join a car pool, but instead she was hand carrying the stupid form around. If she let CPS do it, it would take another month. Car pool services, what a laugh — a two-person department run by a fossil who looked as if he'd become a puddle of crude oil the moment he was buried, and his secretary, who looked as if she did all the work. Shay would have liked to have dipped Mr. Whal-We'll-Get-To-It-As-Soon-As-We-Kin-Missy in the Effluent Ponds and watched him dissolve. But then NOC-U would have taken six months to fill his job with another dinosaur and she still wouldn't have a car pool.

The other potential car poolees were both in the Exec Building. A trip to Executive meant changing out of her usual field clothes into the stupid heels. Well, she'd start with this Anthea Rossignole — what a name, she thought — and if she wasn't there, she'd track down Lois Myers.

She got directions to Rossignole's cube from the finance unit receptionist. 'Who, she noted with a more than a twinge of bitterness, had a nice, quiet space all her own, a computer with about ten times the speed and capacity of the one Shay used, and two perfectly lovely shoes. Heels did look wonderful on some women, but she supposed thinking so was not politically correct. The slender, chocolate brown legs that fit into the shoes were quite nice as well, but Shay was in no mood to linger appreciatively. She didn't have energy to spare for lust.

Shay minced down the aisle between the rows of cubicles, trying to keep her heel from tapping. It was pointless. She felt gauche in the extreme when, to her amazement, she found herself in front of the plate that read Anthea Rossignole. The cubicle was larger than the one she and Harold shared and apparently had only one occupant.

Inside the cube, Shay could only see two dove-gray shoes (she wondered if she was entering a period of shoe envy), matching hose leading up to a rose-gray skirt that covered a shapely behind. For a moment Shay was distracted with the overall niceness of the view. She caught herself just before ... well, almost before ... she officially ogled the unsuspecting woman. The rest of the woman's body was hidden under her workstation and Shay heard a sound she knew too well — a cable sliding just out of reach. The computer monitor flickered out.

"Excuse me," Shay said hesitantly.

"Damn it!" the woman in the cubicle said as the back of her head hit the underside of the workstation. She clambered to her feet, one cable dangling from her hand.

"I'm sorry," Shay said automatically, and then she froze — French Braid! Shay hadn't thought about her since she'd filled in the last square of her time survey sheet. She wondered if French Braid — alias Anthea Rossignole — had found it good reading.

"What — are you from RTS?" Anthea asked, a genuine smile breaking up the angry frown.

"No, I —"

"Oh, wait, haven't we met?" Anthea ran a hand over her hair and smoothed her skirt. Shay wondered why it was that some women could look as if they had just stepped out of a magazine — no one would suspect that Anthea had just been on all fours crawling under her desk.

Shay felt a distinct twinge of contempt as she said, "We met at the GPG trailers."

"Oh, the time survey. You gave me a lift back." Something in her tone told Shay she hadn't forgotten about the dirty truck.

Well, they were off to an amicable start. "I've come about the car pool." Her statement came out as a question somehow.

"You need a car pool? You wouldn't lie about a thing like that, would you?"

"Yes. I mean no. Yes, I need a car pool."

"Would you like some coffee or a Coke?" Anthea's slight frown disappeared completely. The top of Shay's head reached to about the height of Anthea's earlobes. As usual, Shay tipped her head back to carry on the conversation — she'd forgotten that Anthea had seemed tall to her.

"Thanks, but I'm going to be late back from my break," Shay said. It looked like she was going to spend every morning and evening with someone who was moody, even if she was attractive. As if that had anything to do with the ability to drive a car, she told herself. *Gutter brain.* I'm not responsible, she thought. It's sleep deprivation.

"Oh. You know, I never caught your name."

Shay felt herself flush as she remembered how she had deliberately not introduced herself. She hoped it didn't show. Okay, she had been rude, but she still felt a little justified. It was so cloistered and sanitary in the Exec Building. This woman probably had no idea what products and toxic by-products were produced here. "Shay Sumoto. I live in Berkeley, just below campus."

"I'm up near Tilden. Behind the Claremont, but north a bit," Anthea offered. "Do you have the form? I can't wait to sign the thing."

Shay handed it over. It would be lovely to live up above the Berkeley flats in a place that had lots of windows. She saw Anthea's eyes flick over her without a change in her expression, but nevertheless Shay wished she had ironed her skirt. It was worse for wear from being kept in a file cabinet, and it didn't help her mood that it was the skirt she'd bought to wear to her father's funeral — the only skirt she had worn in about ten years.

"Well, we can't get across the Dumbarton for free, but we can sure use the car pool lanes. I'll send this over in the inter-refinery mail," Anthea offered as she put the form down on her desk.

"There's also a Lois Myers who wants to join a car pool, too. We could get out of the bridge toll that way."

Anthea's head jerked up. "I — I've found it's a little harder to coordinate with three people. We can skip the toll by driving through San Jose in the morning and taking the bridge home. A big circle. With the car pool lanes it's a little faster in the morning to take the long way," Anthea said, all in a rush.

Shay saw a red flush creep up Anthea's throat. What brought that on, she wondered. "Okay. Well, we'll see how it goes."

"We should get the pass in about three weeks ... unless the idiot who runs CPS is on vacation." Anthea rolled her eyes and the flush receded.

Shay nodded knowingly. "I know just what you mean. Um, well, even without the pass, we could still drive together, couldn't we? And park in the remote lot. I brought it over so that — could we start as soon as possible, like tomorrow?"

"I'd love to. Commuting alone has been hell. I've been so tempted to risk the hundred-dollar ticket and use the car pool lanes anyway."

"You're sure it's faster to go all the way around in the morning?"

Anthea smiled. Shay remembered the charming expression, but hadn't seen the added nuance of . . . well, something like glee. "Believe me, I've tried all the options." Anthea wriggled her eyebrows knowingly.

Shay swallowed hard. Good lord, her mind was getting soft if she thought this woman was flirting with her. She probably flirted with everyone. "You'll have to show me," Shay said lightly.

"I'll be glad to," Anthea said, her voice returning to its pleasant professional tone. "Where would be the most convenient place to pick you up?"

"Corner of Milvia and University? In front of Luciano's Pizza?"

"Sure, I know where that is. Well," Anthea said briskly, "I should pick you up around six-twenty to be here at half-past seven. That'll give us each time to catch the parking lot shuttle. Oh, here, write down your number on this."

"Okay." Shay scrawled her extension and home phone on the piece of paper Anthea proffered. "This is terrific. See you in the morning." She hurried away, aware of her heel's click, but more concerned with getting back to the field trailers before someone noticed how long she'd been gone. Maybe here no one watched breaks and lunchtime, but the powers that be at their site cared passionately about such things. The fact that she had gotten off on the wrong foot with Anthea, and that she seemed as changeable as helium isotopes, bothered Shay, but not nearly as much as the mere thought of one of Scott's "punctuality is our friend" speeches.

Anthea listened to the dwindling clip-click of Shay's footsteps. Well, well, well, she thought. So we won't be bosom buddies. But at least I have a car pool again. She permitted herself a smile that felt deliciously evil. And Lois doesn't. It had been two months, so she supposed she shouldn't still feel vindictive, but she did. The personnel registry said that Celia no longer worked for NOC-U. Which meant Lois was driving by herself.

She sighed happily, then turned back to her computer. The good feelings seeped away as she resisted the urge to hit it. Taking a deep breath, she got back under the desk and managed to shimmy the cable up between the cube wall and the desktop. It wouldn't work. RTS and their stupid advice. Changing the cabling had nothing to do with the DOS error she was getting.

She flipped the computer on again. After an interminable amount of disk grinding the operating system launched and she gingerly typed in a request for a disk directory.

PARITY.CHECK.50000, the computer said.

The orange cursor went right on blinking in its predictable and perfectly timed way. With each blink of the cursor the machine counted down: 50000 *blink* 49999 *blink* 49998 *blink.* Supposedly, several centuries from now when it reached 00000 *blink,* the computer would be fine. Anthea knew better. She resisted the temptation to use her keyboard to forcibly reconfigure her C drive. Instead she applied a little more force than necessary to the keyboard combination she pressed to warm boot the computer.

Without a disk directory there was no MASTERDB.123, and no report for the boss's boss by two p.m. on the third-quarter operation cost centers. And Martin's boss didn't believe in computer problems. He was convinced that all the accountants had very straightforward computers that didn't break, or could be fixed by inserting a couple of diskettes. *He wouldn't know a computer if one gave him a haircut.*

Methodically, as was her trademark, Anthea began down the list of her options. She didn't care what RTS's advice was.

She replaced the COMMAND.COM file. PARITY.CHECK.50000. 49999. 49998. She warm-booted to try something else.

She replaced the AUTOEXEC.BAT file. PARITY.CHECK.50000. 49999. 49998. Warm boot.

She replaced her major software packages, hoping she didn't wipe out any vital subdirectories. PARITY.CHECK.50000. 49999. 49998. Warm boot again. A cigarette would have really helped her think, but smoking was only permitted in private offices. Smoking in the cubes was not permitted.

Anthea understood why, of course, but she still wished she had a cigarette.

Finally, just short of calling refinery technical support again, she rapped the side of the drive with her ruler and said one of the words she used frequently to describe other drivers during her commute.

"I hear heavy sighs," Adrian said from the other side of the barrier. He sounded sympathetic, but she wasn't fooled. Adrian delighted in the misfortunes of others with an across-the-board-everybody's-equal malice. His total lack of sympathy during her breakup with Lois had probably saved her sanity because, if nothing else, he made her laugh.

"I'm getting a parity check on the C drive. And of course the very next thing I was going to do after this stupid project —"

"— was backup," Adrian said, his voice unmistakably gleeful.

"I spent all of last week on the new data formatting," she admitted. She might as well let him enjoy the whole mess.

"And you didn't do backup? They're paying you too much," Adrian said.

Anthea frowned. "If you have any helpful suggestions, make them. Otherwise," she said, her voice getting snappy, "get back to work."

"Well, if you've already tried the ruler method, I'm no help at all," Adrian said. "Call RTS," was his parting shot. Translated, he meant, "Go screw yourself."

She called RTS again, this time to request service. They were available with their usual rapid-fire response time — six working days. She pleaded for even a trainee to no avail. Technology that had nothing to do with the conversion of crude oil into petroleum products and by-products was a distinct second priority. Besides, everybody knew that computer nerds — Anthea had bitten her tongue when Martin's boss had called her that — could fix their own machines.

"Thanks ever so much." She slammed the phone down. "Technical support, my ass." Anthea realized her foul mouth from the nightmare commute was not limited to the commute anymore.

"Did you get kissed, or are they just going to respect you in the morning?" Adrian's voice carried easily over the divider.

"The least they could do is pretend to care," Anthea said. "I don't suppose you're hungry?"

"If you ordered me to eat, I guess I would have to."

Anthea pursed her lips. "Wrong answer."

Adrian's voice took on a Homer Simpson quality. "Gee, boss, I'd really like to go to lunch now."

Anthea laughed. "That's much better." She got her wallet and then glared at her computer. She hated that an inanimate object could make her feel so helpless. It was bad enough when people made her feel that way.

"This looks absolutely disgusting," Adrian said, referring to his cafeteria tuna medley. "I'd pay full price if they'd improve the quality of the food. Not that I think NOC-U is really underwriting the cost."

"Looks like dinner last night," she said. "I'm so depressed."

"Before or after you ate it? This place is crammed — over here." They settled half behind a pillar partially out of the echoing noise of three hundred or more conversations. "This tastes disgusting, too. I'm getting too old for this kind of food. Not that you would understand."

Anthea smiled at his usual reference to her relative youth. Adrian, at forty-one, often and emphatically reminded her she should respect her elders. She was thirty-four, which made her a child. "I understand plenty. My plaster is completely cast."

"Some study showed that after twenty-nine you can't change anymore," Adrian said. He grimaced as he swallowed more medley. "I feel sorry for you, dear. I get to be an eccentric character, the aging queen. You're just going to be an old —"

"Ssssh! Hush," she said intensely.

"What's wrong with a word? Meanings aren't in words, O Sappha, they're in people."

"I do not want to be the subject of common cafeteria gossip," Anthea said. "It would get back to somebody, you know it would. And I'm not old. Neither are you. And besides, it isn't fair that older men are sex symbols while older women are the butt of jokes. This muffin is old," she added, spreading more butter onto her fingers than the dried-out corn muffin.

"Haven't you heard these are the Gay Nineties?"

"Adrian, please don't," Anthea said. She didn't like being pressured about being in the closet at work. She didn't see Adrian wearing any lavender lambdas. Anyone with eyes to see could tell he was gay, but he didn't advertise it. Anthea, in her suit and heels, was a harder book to read. Given her desire to someday have Martin's job, the last thing she needed was another strike against her. Just being a woman was a big enough strike at NOC-U.

"Ex-cuuse me." Adrian's eyebrows crumpled into an angry vee. His hair seemed to flare. He was offended.

"Sorry," she muttered. "I'm in no mood to be entertained."

"You haven't been in a mood to be entertained for about two months. Ever since what's-her-name left."

"She didn't leave, I threw her out. Just ask the mutual friends who won't speak to me anymore."

"And you've been so happy about it ever since," Adrian said sarcastically. "If you're better off, just get over it, okay? It's getting tedious."

"Thanks for your support," Anthea said, her tone grim.

"There's support and there's indulgence."

"I just need a little more time. I think my moon is in the wrong house or something. God, I hope it's not too late for me to change. I'm still smoking ten cigarettes a day and I want more. The only good thing to happen is getting a car pool again, even if it's with this woman from groundwater protection who thinks she's superior because she works for a living, unlike those of us who just pretend, hiding behind our desks and computers."

Adrian swallowed, then curled his lip. "A person who works for a living, how quaint." He wrinkled his nose.

Anthea laughed. "Some of my best friends work

for a living." What am I saying, she thought suddenly. She didn't have any friends. *Not anymore.* Adrian was her only friend.

The two of them had been in the cost accounting department the longest. They were the two who could never be laid off because they were the two who knew absolutely everything about the costing system. Therefore they worked the longest hours and, because they had so much invested in the system, they were the only ones who cared about the quality of work.

She shrugged philosophically. "It's been since before Christmas, and here it is Valentine's Day. I can put up with anything at this point. I'm glad I found this woman before Lois did. I still can't believe she had the nerve to suggest we go back to car pooling together — after she made me turn in the pass. God, I wish this place was near a BART line. NOC-U couldn't give a shit."

"Disgusting," Adrian said.

"Well, yes it is," she said, flattered by his vehement sympathy. Then she realized he was talking about his tuna surprise.

Anthea was exhausted by the time she pulled into her carport that night. She hauled herself out of the car. Between the computer breakdown and an accident on I-580, she was a dishrag. *Medical emergency — beam me directly to the Bahamas.* At least today was the last day she'd drive alone.

As she fumbled for the key and let herself in, Anthea ignored the little voice that said Shay

Sumoto could be a pain in the ass to commute with. What if Shay's favorite topic was men? Could she really go back to pretending interest, making jokes? She remembered what it had been like with a woman she had car pooled with before Lois and Celia. It had been easy then to nod knowingly about everything from birth control methods to penis sizes. But it had been a while since she'd been forced to pretend.

What if Shay was the kind of person who had confused sexual liberation with license to discuss the most intimate details of her sex life? If she talked about her boyfriend's favorite technique, would Anthea be able to say in response, "I don't need penetration to come. My lover used to make me come with her lips. Just her lips, not even her tongue. And when she did take me, one slender finger could drive me to orgasms that went on for *days*." She started to blush, and knew she could never say anything aloud when just thinking it made her blush. Besides, she wasn't about to admit to anyone that Lois had been a good lover.

Lois, Lois, Lois, she chided herself. *Can't you think about anything else?*

She sighed to herself and went about her routine of hanging up her clothes and making a salad for dinner. Without someone else to cook for she couldn't even indulge her love of working in the kitchen. Brownies from a mix didn't count. The most she managed was salad dressings . . . today she would have lime poppyseed with fresh cilantro.

Olé.

She had only two cigarettes of her half-pack allotment left, and after dinner she savored both of them down to the last ember. She watched TV and thought about exercising while she polished off the rest of a pint of Ben & Jerry's Chunky Monkey. As she let the last bit melt slowly on her tongue, she had a revelation: she didn't miss Lois. She did miss her presence, but she didn't miss her. There seemed to be a major distinction between the two. *This is what a therapist would call a breakthrough.* She set aside the ice cream container and decided it was quicker than therapy even if it was hard on the hips. Adrian had urged her to go again, but she'd had enough for a lifetime . . . first after her parents died, then after the fire. Both of those times she'd been sure therapy would help, but this time she didn't feel like talking to anyone about anything.

Sex had been the only thing that had worked between her and Lois, and that had only worked for a while — not that Anthea had noticed nothing else wasn't working between them. She had thought everything was fine.

She missed stimulating conversation and comforting companionship. She doubted she would get either from Shay Sumoto, who certainly had an attitude. But anything would be better than what she'd been going through. Tomorrow she'd spare a pitying thought for Lois. Feeling pity instead of pain seemed like a step in the right direction.

Shay looked up from her spot at Milvia and University, trying to see if any of the approaching cars was driven by Anthea. She should have asked what kind of car Anthea drove. Something expensive, she suspected. She yawned, despite the extra half-hour sleep she'd given herself. She'd been standing on the corner for almost fifteen minutes, having deliberately arrived early so she could stow a change of clothes in the pizza parlor behind her. For some reason she didn't want Anthea to know she was working two jobs. She didn't want to explain about her father's death and suffer any chance of letting other people see how devastated she still was. That was one reason moving and finding roommates was not an option. There was too much pain yet.

A pale blue Acura Legend was pulling up to the curb — yes, the driver was Anthea. Obviously she was entering Yuppie-land. She buckled up and answered Anthea's smile with one of her own. She hoped it was genuine-looking. Maybe they could just forget about that little incident with the truck.

Anthea asked sweetly, "Need a towel for the seat?"

Or maybe not. Shay felt herself flush a little — hopefully not enough to redden her olive-brown skin, thank goodness — and said, "No, but thanks for the offer."

"You're welcome." Anthea laughed, then said, "Just teasing." She guided the Legend carefully out into traffic. It accelerated evenly and in almost total quiet, Shay thought, unlike her own '81 Horizon.

"Are you always this cheerful in the morning?" Shay stifled a yawn.

"An old roommate used to say I had obnoxious morning disorder."

That about covered it, Shay thought. Anthea was goddamned perky. She realized Anthea was still talking.

"In my last car pool," Anthea went on, "we took turns driving by week."

"Sounds good," Shay said. "I'll make an extra effort to be awake when I'm driving. "

"Well, good, that's settled," Anthea said cheerily. "I'll try to control my good mood in the morning. It's my best time."

Maybe she's an alien, Shay thought. "If you get too obnoxious, I'll ask you to perk down."

"That's a deal," Anthea said.

God, Shay thought. She was relentless with good humor. But they were already onto the freeway and it was too late to bail out of the car. And, before it seemed humanly possible, Anthea was navigating the interchange to I-880 and working her way into the car pool lane which began just north of Hayward. The access roads that led to both the San Mateo and Dumbarton bridges were backed all the way out onto the freeway, but their lane whizzed by without a slowdown.

Anthea turned on the radio to get the traffic update. Shay found shutting out the unending stream of commercials easy — she was used to shutting out voices in the crowded field trailer. Especially men's voices talking about their wives and girlfriends in disgusting terms. When one man had insisted that "happiness was a sticky crotch," she had wanted to throw up. She had a very strong suspicion that he wouldn't know what to do with a sticky crotch if he fell into one face first. Thank the heavens that Harold was a decent sort and didn't join in on the guy talk.

She distracted herself from anticipating the horrors of another working day by looking at the landscaping. Until now she had never really appreciated the ice plant California's transportation department placed along the embankments at the freeway overcrossings. She knew the motive was erosion control, but just now, as the soil began to soften for spring, the ground was dusted with pale lavender and vibrant rose. She was going to like car pooling. It gave her a chance to look around her for a change.

Anthea finally got a report that told her it was all clear on the 880-280 crossover and she switched off the radio. "So Shay, what exactly do you do for NOC-U and goundwater protection?"

Shay looked slightly startled, as if she had been thinking about something else. Anthea was sorry she had intruded on her thoughts. "I'm a field geologist," Shay said.

Anthea arched her eyebrows and glanced at her passenger. "Really?"

"I don't look the part?" Shay sounded half amused, half-angered by Anthea's surprise.

"Most of the field geologists are men," Anthea said.

"Tell me about it," Shay said. "I'm the only female field geologist on the site."

Anthea gave a little nod of acknowledgment as she changed lanes. "I'll admit I haven't processed the time survey sheets completely, so I'm not exactly sure what a field geologist does." Not that she'd had time and it wasn't as if Reed would do it since Ruben was gone.

"We dig holes, install wells, take samples and perform analysis on the data." Shay stopped.

"For . . . ?"

"Gee, you're actually interested," Shay said. "At this point most people are asleep. Well, groundwater samples are taken all over the refinery. They're analyzed and the results are mapped to trace the movement of certain constituents . . . chemicals."

"Why groundwater? Wouldn't soil be more accurate?"

"Well, a groundwater sample can be two types. One type comes from wells, and the other from soil borings which, of course, are soil mixed with water. In both cases, it what's dissolved in the water that matters. Xylene, for example, can't spontaneously come to life in soil. It has to get there by some method. The production of petroleum-based products and chemicals has a lot of by-products, most of which are on the hazardous substances list. They leak into the groundwater because of rain, or pipe breakage — whatever — and the groundwater moves through the soil, carrying the toxics with it. So we're tracking how the groundwater is moving and whether any toxic constituents are reaching public waters, like the bay, for example. It's not too far to the wildlife refuge on the eastern shore."

Anthea said, "I'm not telling any secrets if I tell you GPG's way over budget."

"Not on account of my salary," Shay muttered, then she grinned at Anthea, who threw her a smile.

"You'll be good for me," Anthea said. "I very often forget what we make at the NOC-U hell hole."

"Now, now," Shay said in a mocking tone.

"Remember that National's image is important even among ourselves."

Anthea couldn't decide if Shay was serious. She smiled noncommittally. Either Shay had been to too many safety meetings or she had no illusions about NOC-U's relentless cheerleading. Anthea had forgotten how annoying she had initially found the meetings, just like she'd forgotten they were supposed to say National, not Knock-You.

To fill the silence, Anthea said, "I'm having a horrible time with my computer."

"What's it doing?" Shay's voice alternated between sleepy and alert.

"Parity check. I've replaced my batch files, the command.com and autoexec.bat and I think I'm going to have to reinitialize and lose all my files."

"Don't do that," Shay said. "Use Norton to recover a file . . . any file. See if that helps."

"Why would that make a difference?"

"It might reset the root directory."

Anthea started to gape, but turned her head away to wave at the guard at Gate 12. What did a field technician know about computers?

Anthea looked at the car clock as she turned off the engine. "Sixty-five minutes, not bad if I say so myself."

"Definitely," Shay said. Anthea watched as Shay scrambled out of the low seat with a lot less fuss than Anthea did. Shay was . . . lithe. There was no other word for it. Anthea picked up her satchel and promised herself to lose five pounds as soon as possible. Then she mentally erased the promise — trying to lose weight was the surest way she'd found to gain it. She was better off promising to exercise, but then she reminded herself she was concentrating on quitting smoking. She realized she hadn't wanted a cigarette during the entire drive, which gave her a really good feeling. She waved goodbye to Shay, who headed for the outbound shuttle stop, and then walked toward her inbound shuttle stop. She could see the little bus chugging its way toward her.

When she got to her computer she remembered Shay's advice. Well, maybe a field technician had unknown skills. She booted off her Norton recovery disk and recovered a small file. She turned the computer off again and crossed her fingers. "Look, you piece of junk, my life is improving. You load or I'm getting a Macintosh." She flipped the power toggle.

After a lengthy amount of grinding disk noise, she was able to get a directory and backup her files, then reinitialize her drive. She would have to tell Shay they were even over the nasty truck incident. It would take the better part of the day to reinstall Windows and her software, but she was well on her way. She shared her morning muffin with Adrian when he joined her for a congratulatory cup of coffee.

"You're just lucky," he said. "Better call RTS and cancel the call or they'll show up and break the thing again."

"Good idea. What do you think of the muffin?"

"Love," he said gently, "I know the cooking is therapy, but what possessed you to put pearl onions in a cranberry muffin?"

Anthea was devastated. "Well, you don't have to eat it. Buy your own."

"Can't afford it," he said. "I'll just pick out the onions. Did you cut the recipe out of the paper or something?"

Anthea sniffed. *"Gourmet Magazine,* if you please." She took another bite, then picked out an onion. "I do think they're . . . an acquired taste."

"Tell you what," Adrian said. "When payday finally rolls around I'll treat you to blueberry muffins from paradise. I get them at a little bakery on Castro."

Anthea finished her muffin and threw away her accumulated pile of pearl onions. "I have to get back to the Castro someday." *Maybe it's time I did.*

"You make it sound like you have to see a travel agent to do it. I'd be thrilled to be your guide," Adrian said. "You do smell faintly of mothballs."

Anthea pursed her lips at him, adding her best glare. He went away.

3

Slow Merge

Shay carefully stepped to the very edge of the plywood plank. She knelt slowly, maintaining her balance. Today's field buddy was her cube mate, Harold. He was on the other end, providing stability for the plank. Even though she was in a Level D protective suit with breather, and would not step directly on the soil underneath the plank, Shay was feeling paranoid. She tried to work quickly, but the soil sample had to be perfect. There was no room for sloppiness. And then she had to draw a water sample from Well B-A-146, a well she had installed herself the first week on the job.

The immediate area was barren of any form of life — not even a weed or fallen leaf. The soil was cracked and it varied from a pasty gray ash to a coppery clay. When they left they would drive under and next to scaffolds riddled with pipes and conduit. Some of the pipes were flare points, and the flashes of flame created images of hell for Shay. It stretched on for a couple square miles.

She drew the water sample out of the well, completed the label and added it to the Styrofoam cooler, which would maintain an even temperature for all the samples until they were taken to the lab that afternoon. She put her tools away, made sure everything was in place, then stood again, giving the "move out" signal to Harold, who stepped lightly forward and lifted the cooler easily. Shay had no trouble believing that he had, as he said, played football for the USC Trojans.

Harold grinned at her after he put the cooler in the truck and held up one finger. Shay nodded vigorously and pantomimed wiping her brow. Only one more sample, and it was the least contaminated spot on their trip. They repeated procedures again at Well B-B-146. As she drew the water sample, she asked herself if NOC-U could have found a more confusing way to label the wells — they were just asking for mislabeled containers. When she was finished, they went back to the truck, drove past the hydrogen disulfide boundary, and stopped again. Shay bailed out of the truck and yanked her breather off.

"Air. Honest to goodness polluted air." She sucked in a couple of rapid breaths and felt her nerves calm.

"I think this is how they get us to believe this is clean air," Harold said. "I'm always so glad to breathe in this shit that I think it's clean." His last words were muffled as he pulled the top of his Tyvek suit over his head.

Shay knew that nine in ten women would be going ape for Harold. He was a cross between Roger Craig and O.J. Simpson, with all of their good looks and engaging smiles. He had flawless deep brown skin, close-cropped hair and eyes that always said, "I'm listening, you're important." Shay liked him a lot — but her feelings were based on the way he approached life and treated people, not his looks.

She'd been at this stage — suit removal — with lots of other field "buddies." It didn't matter that she had clothes on underneath. It felt like undressing and after some of the other men had watched her taking her suit off she'd learned to stay on her side of the truck. She'd had enough leering. And she was always glad when she was paired with Harold because Harold treated her like a human being. Nor did he ignore her gender and race, just as she couldn't ignore his. When two people are getting to know each other, gender and color are facts of life. When it came to taking well samples and borings they didn't matter at all. Now that they were spending a lot of time together, enough to approach friendship, Shay was trying to find a way to let Harold know she was a lesbian. If she could tell Mrs. Giordano, she could tell Harold. She wondered if she'd ever tell Anthea. Maybe. She couldn't really picture herself being friends with Anthea.

They filled the decontamination pool, actually a child's plastic wading pool, with three inches of nonpotable water from the decontamination station faucet. They waded around until their boots were free of any soil they had picked up. They dumped the water and put the pool and their suits in the back of the truck. Shay took off her boots and added them to the pool, and then padded to the passenger seat again. Harold was already lacing on his Nikes.

"Let's take the scenic route," Shay said. "I don't know about you, but if we never got back to the trailers it would be too soon."

"I was eating this really cheap ice cream last night — chocolate chip. There were about six chocolate chips in the entire half gallon and that's when I realized that I'm a chocolate chip in this cheap vanilla company."

Shay laughed. "Does that make me toffee?"

"There's more of your people than mine in this place," Harold said with a shrug. He started the truck and it slowly moved down the roadway.

"Yeah, but I'm the only one not doing statistics and accounting. They hire Asians at NOC-U but only to do things that Asians are supposedly so good at. There aren't any Asians in product development and no team leaders."

Harold chewed his lip. "I hadn't noticed that. You're right. So why do we put up with this place?"

Shay laughed. "How much do you have in your savings account?"

"What savings account?"

"Exactly. I had thought that the old boys' network was dying out, but it's alive and well here."

Harold stopped to let a truck filled with soil cross in front of them. Shay stared after it, then shook her head. They moved a lot of soil around on this refinery.

Harold said, "It is there, isn't it? I thought it was me. I'll be walking along and get the feeling I've crossed a line I wasn't supposed to cross —"

"Like a force field or something. I feel it too. You just know you're an alien being. Around here anyone who isn't a straight white man over fifty is an alien — oh, women who wear skirts and type and file all day aren't aliens either, as long as they call their boss Mister. And believe me, I noticed the only black women in this place are clerical workers."

"You'd think after working on a refinery for twenty-five years, some of these guys would have died off. Let's hope they're not breeding."

"Actually, it isn't an age thing," Shay said. "Look at Scott. He's what, thirty-five? Mr. Roger Ramjet. And you're the only guy who so far has asked me if I wanted to drive. The rest just assumed I would be the passenger — even the guys who are my age."

"My momma'd slap me upside the head when I got out of line. She always said a son of hers would learn respect for women or die young."

"That accounts for that pointy head you have."

"Who are you calling pointy? That's rich coming from a pee-wee like you."

They happily traded insults about each other and then about the more obnoxious people at the trailers as Harold wended their way back to the main roads. They could talk freely here, unlike in their cube

66

where every word they said could be heard by a half dozen other people.

Harold pulled into the cafeteria lot since it was close to lunch. Shay felt a warm wave of relaxation and realized she'd been walking around tensed up every day. Maybe she'd sleep deeper and better for knowing someone shared her views of the place.

"Wait a second," she said, when Harold started to open his door. "Since I think this is the beginning of a beautiful friendship, I want you to know that I'm gay."

She was sure Harold would be fine about it — screw him if he wasn't — but his response floored her. He flashed her a brilliant smile and said, "Did you think you were the only one? It'll be nice to have a real buddy."

She smiled back — a long, slow smile that didn't fade until well after lunch.

"Do you think that all used Volvos are shipped straight to Berkeley?" Shay slowed for a school crossing. Anthea was sitting quietly in the passenger seat, something Shay took for confidence in her driving. Anthea didn't brake reflexively, which was also nice. In spite of Anthea's complete lack of understanding about what actually happened on an oil refinery, her flawless elegance, easy charm and obvious financial means, Shay was beginning to like her.

"Actually, I've often thought that."

Shay's Horizon gathered itself and managed to pass a yellow Volvo that Shay privately thought was the color of a baby's used diaper. "I mean, you never see brand-new Volvos in Berkeley, do you?"

"Never."

"Only used Volvos."

"Only used."

Shay peeked a look at Anthea as she braked for a light. Anthea was grinning. "What's so funny?"

"I thought I was the only one who saw it. The Volvo Conspiracy. I think it's something in the water."

"Nah, it's just that the owners don't want to be thought snobs, but a Volvo is politically correct. So they buy a used Volvo."

"Maybe they buy them new and hide them in a garage for a couple of years, then dent the passenger door with a blunt instrument — No, no, you jerk!," Anthea exclaimed.

"I knew it," Shay said. "Another used Volvo." The green car made a hurried right turn in front of them, *Baby on Board* sign swaying, forcing Shay to slam on the brakes. The Volvo then slowed to thirty miles an hour. "I know it's the speed limit, but it's rush hour." Shay moaned. "That means you're supposed to rush!" She squeezed between a bus and a garbage truck, both of which were outstripping the Volvo by about two miles an hour. Another inch, another inch — she yanked her Horizon over in front of the Volvo and sped down University to the freeway onramp.

The Volvo honked. Anthea applauded. With precision timing they both gave the Volvo the finger. Shay looked over at Anthea and they giggled like teenagers.

Anthea said, "Have you ever noticed you'll do things in your car that you won't do anywhere else?"

Shay gave a stifled shout of laughter as she merged into the slowly progressing traffic. "I figured that out in high school. I've done things in the back of a car I don't think I'll ever do anywhere else." She laughed more and looked over at Anthea.

Anthea laughed too, but Shay realized she had sounded . . . like she'd been . . . easy. She frowned at herself. What a horrible high school word, she thought. Making out with another girl in the back seat of a car had been anything *but* easy.

"Me too. I have fond memories of back seats," Anthea said unexpectedly. She turned her attention back to her book. Something by Jane Austen — Shay hadn't been able to catch the title. For the last month it had been Proust, but before that she'd been reading a sci-fi series Shay had also enjoyed, so Anthea wasn't completely stuffy. She liked *Star Trek,* for instance, which gave them something to talk about besides the weather. Anthea had her moments.

Shay adroitly missed the two potholes lurking in the Emeryville curve. She was glad she hadn't offended Anthea. The fog was lifting to make way for moist spring heat. It would continue to warm up into June, Anthea had said, then the fog would come in and it would be summer in San Francisco.

Anthea murmured, "God, it's a beautiful city. It always looks so fresh and clean in the morning."

"I like Berkeley, but I wish I could afford to live in the city." She kept her eyes on the traffic, but stole glances at the tiers of hills behind and south of the skyscrapers marking the financial district. She'd driven around the Noe Valley and Mission neighborhoods. Some were pretty bad, some were pretty nice, but they were all part of an amalgam of people who looked different. The kind of people she never saw at the refinery. The kind of people who looked alive. She'd been in more countries and American cities than she could count. New York had been home base for much of her youth, but San Francisco had caught her fancy.

She lost sight of the city as they merged onto 580. They chugged past an ancient VW minivan that was plastered with stickers bearing slogans like "Promote Homosexuality" and "Queer is Here." Well, that was another reason she liked the Bay Area. Shay liked all the gay people. She saw Anthea glance at, then away from the minivan, and wondered, not for the first time, what Anthea would think if she knew Shay was a lesbian. Anthea seemed so . . . unreachable that Shay was sure they'd never discuss it.

Given the fun they'd had flipping off the Volvo, maybe Anthea wasn't as square as she seemed. She'd just found out yesterday that Anthea was 34. She looked 34, but Shay had thought she looked young for her age — lots of good makeup could do that — somewhere near 40 from the way she acted. No way did she think Anthea was only six years older than herself.

If they weren't in the car pool would Shay ever consider making a friend of Anthea? They spent a lot of time together and it was slow going getting to know her. It probably would have been too much of an effort if she'd met Anthea at the supermarket or the library. About once a week they would do something — like flipping that Volvo off — that was in complete harmony, as if they'd known each other for a long time. And sometimes they'd have conversations that touched on more than the weather, food and *Star Trek* — although Anthea's conversations about food bordered on the deliciously obscene and orgiastic. Shay guessed she was a heck of a chef. But on just about any other topic Anthea had a wall around her that Shay respected. She understood wanting privacy.

Traffic slowed to a sedate fifty as drivers spotted a CHP car on the shoulder up ahead. Shay gave up the complex thinking and concentrated on survival.

During Memorial Day weekend, it came to Anthea that she was turning into a mushroom. Except for the necessities of shopping, she never went anywhere. She'd even turned her ballet tickets back to the box office as a donation so they could sell them again. Was she just sitting around waiting for something to happen? She refused to think that subconsciously she was waiting for Lois to come back. Maybe she was waiting for something else to fill up some of the hole Lois had left. Granted she looked forward to work more since she'd been able to hire another analyst, and to the car pool and talking to Shay. But wasn't life supposed to be more than that? It had been nearly six months since she had broken up with Lois and those ties were still there, like Jacob Marley's chains, weighing Anthea down until she could hardly move.

On Saturday afternoon, she found herself

considering reading *Pride and Prejudice* again. That or *Anna Karenina* — now that would certainly cheer her up. She had finally managed to wade through the Proust she'd told herself to read just about all her life. She clicked through all sixty-three cable channels, watched an episode of Perry Mason she'd seen before and ate a box of crackers, then enjoyed two of her remaining eight cigarettes for the day. She let herself sigh over Della Street, whom she'd had a crush on since she was twelve or so. The fact that she was still smoking really depressed her. She thought she'd be able to drop off two cigarettes a month and by now, she'd have just about kicked the habit.

As she shuffled back into the kitchen to forage for more junk food, she realized she felt cooped up and stifled. She never went anywhere anymore. What's the matter, she asked herself. Afraid you'll run into Lois? The least she could do was go to the library. She hadn't been in weeks, and then it was just to toss the books into the return deposit. Well, it would be something to do and she could pick up a burger on the way home. As if, she told herself, she didn't have time to cook.

An hour later, after spending too much time deciding how one should dress for the library, Anthea strolled between aisles of fiction. She pulled books she had read from the shelves, put them back, and wondered what she might like to read that was new and exciting . . . anything to make Saturday nights shorter.

As she turned the corner, a thin, tall trade paperback caught her eye. She casually read the title, then casually slid it off the shelf. She turned away from the rest of the aisle for maximum privacy and examined the back cover. Yes, it was a novel for lesbians. And she hadn't read it.

She glanced over at the checkout counter. A woman who looked just like the librarian at her junior high school was working there. She couldn't just check out one book ... could she? Maybe she should look for some others. But she wanted to rush right home and read this book. Hurriedly, she gathered a few mysteries she'd read a long time ago. She carefully hid the trade paperback among the other books and then waited in line at the counter. It's the Gay Nineties, she told herself.

When she reached the front of the line she handed the stack over and held her breath. A few moments later, the librarian handed the entire stack back with a mere "happy reading." No significant eye contact, no disapproval.

Gees, Andy, what did you expect? This is Berkeley, *for God's sake.*

She picked up a burger at Oscar's on the way home, then spent the remainder of the day on the sofa. She devoured the book — she wanted more. It had been a while since she'd read any fiction for lesbians. She'd go back to the library after work on Tuesday. Heck, she could just run over to Boadecia's Books. Just because she'd only gone there with Lois didn't mean she couldn't go by herself.

Sunday was looking to be tedious, so Anthea knuckled down and cleaned. She got down on her hands and knees and scrubbed the laundry room floor — something she hadn't done in a year at least, and Lois's running shoes had left black marks everywhere. She applied every ounce of pressure she could to the marks and realized she was scrubbing away Lois, not the black marks. Well, the black marks came off too, but every one of them was Lois. It had been too many months and Anthea finally felt as if she was free of needing Lois.

If I had a daughter, Anthea thought, I'd give her one piece of advice: never date or sleep with anyone you meet in a support group, even after the support group is over. She'll know too much about all your buttons. Lois, she knew, had pushed them all.

She sat back and studied the floor. She could eat off it now. Her shoulders ached, but she was a woman with a mission.

Anthea decided it was time for an extermination which required stamping every bit of Lois's essence from every corner of the house for personal health and safety reasons. She'd spent nearly a half a year in a blue funk. *No more moping!* In addition to good old-fashioned dusting, scrubbing and vacuuming, she cleaned out the closets, organized the pots and pans, and threw away every piece of Tupperware that did not have a functional lid. She consolidated multiple cans of the same spices into one and then organized them alphabetically. Lois had said her spice rack was anal retentive and Anthea had believed her. Now she decided there was nothing wrong with organized spices, not when you cooked a lot. Her conscience reminded her that she hadn't really cooked anything in six months.

To her eyes, as she looked around, everything was shining and bright, almost as it had been after construction had finished. Her nose, which smelled more scents now that she smoked less, appreciated the aroma of furniture polish. She could think of the

fire and starting over without a wrench of pain —
that was thanks to the support group, just to be
fair. A support group for lesbians who had lost
everything in the fire had brought Lois into her life.
When they had realized that Lois also worked for
NOC-U, having dinner, then car pooling, then
sleeping together, then living together — it had
seemed like fate. Hah, Anthea thought.

Nearly six months was long enough to recover
from Lois. She'd gotten over the fire faster than
that. She'd worked out the strongest of her mixed
love-hate feelings about her parents in less than
that. It was time to get over Lois. And, just because
the house smelled so nice after she'd vacuumed the
carpet freshener up, she decided she wouldn't smoke
in the house anymore. She'd only smoke outdoors.
She'd been trying to quit since New Year's . . . it was
time to finish the job. She fell into bed exhausted
and slept better than she had in weeks.

She used her holiday to reward herself, so she
made an extravagant trip to Macy's at Hilltop — it
was White Flower Day — and returned with new
kitchen towels, linens and comforter for the bed,
bath towels, and a silk plant for the table in the
foyer. She had chosen less exotic colors and patterns
than Lois would have, but screw Lois, she thought.
She neatly packed several boxes of brilliant-hued
linens and wrote herself a note to call the Salvation
Army tomorrow. Bye bye, Lois.

She sat down on a low ottoman to assess her
last big job. The albums and CDs were a mess,
partly because Lois's had been removed willy-nilly
and partly because Lois had never bothered to file
back anything she removed. Anthea pressed her lips

together. Okay, maybe organizing spices was not essential, but Lois had actually implied Anthea was anal retentive for wanting her music organized. Suddenly awash with fury, she pulled all the CDs off the shelves and began stacking them by classification. Bach was the start of one stack, with the Tallis Scholars and Paganini, but not REO Speedwagon or the Police — they went in the Rock stack — was that too much to ask? And Teresa Trull and Bonnie Raitt and Sweet Honey in the Rock were in a class by themselves, not just hodgepodged in with the GoGos and the Carpenters — was that too much to ask? Was it too much to ask for order and just a bit of discipline?

Halfway down the stack she found one of Lois's CDs: Hall & Oates' *Greatest Hits*. *How did I actually sleep with a person who owned this?* She took the CD out to the garage and set it down on the small workbench. Bye bye, Lois.

It only took one whack with a hammer to bust the case and two more to mangle the CD completely.

Well. That felt better than a bataka bat on a pillow. She dumped the pieces into the garbage can.

A couple of hours later she forced herself to stop smiling because her face was actually beginning to hurt. She wished she knew how to whistle. Lauren Bacall had made it sound so easy.

"How was your day?" Anthea buckled up and started the car, immediately pressing the control for air-conditioning. The car interior was searing hot after sitting in the sun all day. Shay smiled her answer as she buckled herself in, wincing as the heat penetrated her thin T-shirt. She resisted the temptation to close her bleary eyes.

She could easily let the heat relax her muscles and drop off to sleep. Anthea handled the car so smoothly and competently that Shay had often been able to sleep on the way to work without a single disturbed moment. The extra half hour or so was keeping her alive. But sleeping on the way home, too . . . well, that seemed rude and it made her groggy at the pizza parlor. So she held her eyes open wide and watched Anthea's hands on the wheel, not gripping too tightly or too casually. Smooth, controlled. She wondered if Anthea was always that smooth.

Shay blinked several times and realized where her silent musings were drifting. She had promised herself that she wouldn't do this. It just wasn't appropriate, nor did it have any chance of coming to fruition. Still, Anthea was easy on Shay's tired eyes. She tried to remember why she had initially disliked Anthea.

She hadn't had a lover since Kuwait — a tempestuous affair with an engineer who, after the job finished, had gone back to the girlfriend she'd finally told Shay existed. Shay hadn't really been upset. Her father and her career had absorbed all her time. Maybe that had been the wrong thing to do. Without her father, it had all just slipped through her fingers.

And for months now, she had been spending two hours each day with, in Shay's humble and lustful opinion, this womanly-soft and attractive person. Still, Anthea was not her type. She was a Yuppie

77

for starters. And not in the least political. And not possibly a lesbian, something that really was key to a successful affair. She was only thinking this way because they spent so much time together — it was inevitable, yet inappropriate. Besides, Shay told herself sternly, she had other things to think about.

Like the two paychecks in her fanny pack. Shay sighed. Her libido catalyzed from a helium isotope to lead. They totaled just over twelve hundred. Somehow, when she'd taken this job, she'd thought the pizza parlor would be just temporary. Just a few more months. Well, it had been a few more months. She'd even worked Memorial Day. She tried to add up her finances and make the reality come out differently. Four hundred for rent, fifty for water and utilities. Eight hundred left. Two fifty for the car payment, one hundred for food — peanut butter and jelly was her staple — about one hundred for gas and insurance. That left three hundred.

And that was fifty bucks short of what her first-of-the-month pay had to contribute to the middle-of-the-month checks for the hospital and funeral bills. Her tip money would probably just cover the gap as usual, but that meant no movies or paperbacks, which is what her tip money usually went for. She went over the numbers again in her head. The bottom line remained unchanged. A couple of hours of overtime at the refinery would have made all the difference, but there had been a month-long moratorium on that. She chewed the inside of one cheek and tried not to resent Anthea. The Legend's hubcaps would probably cover a month's rent.

It was the absence of motion that woke her. "I'm sorry," she mumbled as she scrambled out of the car.

"It's okay," Anthea said. "You look beat."

"I'll give myself an extra hour's sleep tonight," Shay said. She wondered what Anthea thought made her so tired — she had never found a chance to explain about her second job. She wasn't quite sure why she didn't want to talk about it. Probably because it would underscore the differences between them. And because she didn't want pity or sympathy. Not from anyone. She could barely swallow it from Mrs. Giordano. She waved Anthea away, and waited until her car was out of sight before she went into the pizza parlor, got the satchel she'd left that morning and slowly changed. She tied a serviceable apron around her waist and went to make herself a salad before the dinner rush. The free food was the only thing that kept her from complaining about the lack of breaks and an adequate rest area.

She had only two more monthly payments to the hospital and funeral home to scrape together, and then she'd finally be out from under the bills. And then she'd work this job a little longer to have some savings to call her own and then — oh happy day — she'd quit. And she'd do things with her evenings and her Saturdays. The mere thought felt almost as good as sex. Suddenly she thought of Anthea, which disconcerted her. She made herself think about what bliss it would be to quit NOC-U. Anthea slipped out of her head again, which was a relief.

Maybe she wouldn't resent working at NOC-U so much if she weren't assigned to a supervisor whose lazy methodology covered an astounding lack of scientific knowledge. Only Harold kept her from committing gross insubordination several times a week. Most of the bosses in the trailer didn't know bay mud from bedrock. But they all had a private secretary and a company car.

Her father's two brothers had offered to help with the funeral expenses, but Shay couldn't, on principle, take their money. Not only did Shay not know them, but they hadn't spoken to her father for thirty years. Besides, they had wanted to bury him in the family plot and her father's wish had been to have his ashes scattered from an airplane so he could join Shay's mother, he said, in riding the wind. So, instead of healing and letting go, Shay constantly thought about him and how he died. And at night — God, how she was tired of the smell of oregano in her hair.

For a moment, she imagined Anthea's elegantly coifed coil of red-gold hair and couldn't, for the life of her, imagine it smelling like oregano. It probably smelled like rose silk or water lilies. Most likely it smelled like smoke. The thought dampened her libido completely. Cigarettes had killed her father. She realized she was thinking about him again.

She looked down at the congealing cheese and pepperoni oil on the pizza for Table 3. She was tired.

4

Speed Bump

"So my parents wanted to kiss up to this wealthy great-aunt and stuck me with *Anthea*. Very British."

"Did the great-aunt come across with the inheritance?" Shay glanced sideways at Anthea with eyebrows raised as she downshifted for the light at University and San Pablo. Shay looked exhausted, Anthea realized.

"No, she gave it all to a wastrel nephew — at least that's what my parents called him." She didn't add that in retrospect she suspected he was gay. She paused. "So, I told you my story, now you have to tell me about how you were named Shay."

"Well, my father loved baseball. I think I told you he was a consulting geologist and we moved around a lot. Baseball was a mania in Dad's life. On their first date he took my mom to a Mets game. So she had a fondness for the stadium."

"So?" Anthea prompted.

"Well, when I was just about to make my appearance, they were still living in New York. My mom was tired of waiting for me to show up, so they went to a Mets game. And she went into labor during the seventh inning stretch. The facilities people rushed her to the hospital and I popped out pretty quickly, about nine months and ten minutes after the wedding, as the saying goes. My dad had been relegated to the waiting room and they'd agreed my mom should name me whatever she felt at the time. He didn't want to carry on any of his family names for reasons I won't bore you with." Shay stopped as if Anthea would realize a joke was coming. "So she named me after the stadium."

Anthea frowned. "But . . . Shea Stadium is spelled differently, isn't it? I don't follow sports much, but. . . ."

"You're right," Shay said. "That's the joke of my name. My dad was in the waiting room, so she told the nurse. And the nurse evidently didn't know baseball, because she spelled it wrong on the birth certificate."

"You're making it up."

"It's a true story," Shay said, with a wide grin. "Dad said when they were waiting for the second baby they joked about doing the same thing again. Name the kid a version of Wrigley, or some such thing."

"I didn't know you had a brother. Or is it a sister?"

"I don't," Shay said. "The baby and my mom didn't make it through delivery."

"And your dad died recently, didn't he," Anthea said quietly, regretting her tactless remark. "I'm sorry."

"Lung cancer. He smoked three packs a day from the time he was fourteen." Shay's voice revealed ill-concealed bitterness.

"I'm trying to quit," Anthea said. "I haven't made much progress. I'm still at a half a pack." She saw Shay's quick look, and could tell Shay was on the verge of delivering an anti-smoking lecture. She braced herself.

"It cost forty-five thousand dollars for him to die. Four months in intensive care. What insurance didn't cover wiped out everything we'd saved. I'm still paying the bills." Shay's mouth snapped shut, as if she were trying to hold back more details. She glanced out the window and Anthea saw her chest expand with a deep breath. "Going to do anything exciting this weekend?"

Okay, we'll change the subject, Anthea thought. "No, but I'm still glad it's Friday," she said, "Aren't you?"

"I'm determined to finish this series of books I've been working on for almost three weeks now. I have to get to the library on Sunday," Shay said.

"I just started going to the library again. I'd forgotten how good the selection is." She negotiated her car into the red zone across the street from Luciano's. "See you Monday," she said, as Shay scrambled out of the car. Anthea turned up Shattuck toward the library.

A short while later, she was happily supplied with a Mercedes Lackey book Shay had recommended and two more novels with lesbian characters — a mystery and a romance. She was trying to decide if she needed to hunt for something more when someone said, "That's a really good book. The one on top."

She turned toward the voice to find a young woman regarding her with a pleasant smile. A labrys dangled from one ear. Anthea said, "Oh, good. I'm looking forward to reading it. The plot seemed very interesting."

"I guessed who did it right away. Just don't believe a word the older brother has to say. He's such a sleaze."

Anthea blinked. "Did you just tell me who did it?"

"You would have known from page two anyway."

"But that's a terrible thing to do to somebody," Anthea said. She looked down at the book with something like pain. "Now it's spoiled."

"Hey, I'm sorry," the other woman said. "It's still worth reading. Maybe I can make it up to you." Anthea glanced up, her mouth slightly open. The woman laughed. "That sounded like a pickup, didn't it?"

"Sort of."

"Well, it was."

Little butterflies zipped around in Anthea's stomach. She suddenly recalled the aroma of pizza wafting out of Luciano's near where she dropped Shay every night. Somehow she found the nerve to say, "I was going to go have a pizza. Would you like to split one?"

"Okay." Brown eyes, Anthea thought. Pretty eyes. "My name's Paula. Paula McCarthy."

"I'm Anthea Rossignole. I know, it's French for nightingale. I'll just go check out these books."

They walked to Anthea's car, then decided they shouldn't try to relocate it with parking in Berkeley being what it was, so they left their books in the car and walked several blocks to the pizza parlor. Since it was still early, they claimed the table at the window.

"There's a movie with an evil character in it who goes around tearing the last page out of mysteries," Anthea said.

"That's depraved." Paula smiled and it crinkled into her eyes. "I really am sorry I blew the ending of your book."

"I'll get over it." She studied the menu card to avoid looking at Paula. God, she was cute. Or maybe, Anthea thought, it had just been a very long time since she'd had a date or anything else, for that matter.

Someone placed napkins and cutlery on the table and Anthea glanced up. "Shay!" she said, startled.

"Hi," Shay answered. Anthea realized Shay was embarrassed. So was she. "What're you two having?"

It was an innocent question, but Anthea started to blush from her shoulders and it swooped to the top of her head. Shay glanced at Paula's labrys earring, her close-cropped hair and the tiny tattoo of a triangle on the back of one wrist. She saw Shay

85

smile. Then, she saw Shay wink. Shay's smile got wider and she quirked an eyebrow knowingly. Anthea's heartbeat went into warp drive.

Apparently unaware of Anthea's complete discomfiture, Paula ordered a vegetarian pizza and a pitcher of beer. "I'm really hungry."

"I'll have iced tea," Anthea said, adding, "I don't drink."

"I learn something new about you every day," Shay observed innocently, but her smile was ear to ear. She made a note on her order pad and looked back at Paula. "Is that it?"

"Oh, I'll skip the beer, then." Paula wrinkled her nose in an adorable, endearing way that said Anthea's wishes meant something to her. "I'll have some iced tea too."

Shay nodded, then hurried away after another wink at Anthea. Anthea said the first thing that came into her head. "Do you do this often?"

"Why do you ask?"

"You seem pretty, uh, practiced." Anthea hoped it was a smile on her face.

"Well, let's put it this way. It's tough to meet dykes. When I do, I follow up on it. There's a lot of women out there who'd like a casual relationship with someone like me."

Anthea managed to catch her jaw before it hit the table. She wanted to laugh. *Arrogant little piece of shit, isn't she?* "So, that's the offer? Casual relationship? Between someone like me and someone like you." Okay, she thought, I'm probably ten years older, and thirty pounds heavier. But really.

Paula leaned forward with an air of intimacy. "Look, I'm not into territory or monogamy and happy-ever-after. I've found that . . . older women usually are. I just want to make it clear what my priorities are. I like sex. All kinds."

"All kinds of what? People?"

"No, no, I'm pure dyke. No men. Christ, they get an erection and they think the whole world's dying to revolve around it." She laughed. "No, I meant all kinds of dynamics." Paula ran her gaze over Anthea and bit her lower lip in a sexy fashion that made Anthea stare at their soft redness. It had been a long time. Her thighs clenched. Paula went on, "Lately I've been appreciating pure vanilla. It's very sweet. Very safe. Very satisfying." She laughed again.

What on earth was she talking about, Anthea wondered. Could ten years make that much of a communication difference? Shay delivered plates and iced teas. Anthea stared up at her in bemusement.

Shay looked as if she was trying very hard not to laugh. "Your pizza will be up in a few minutes. Do you want some garlic bread while you wait?"

Paula said, "Sure, why not?" Shay nodded and Paula watched as she walked away. "You must come here a lot," she said.

"Why is that?"

"You know *her.* I've been trying to strike up a conversation with her for the last month. She always told me she was too tired for anything, and here you know her name." Paula looked at Anthea as if she would have to reconsider Anthea's skills. Just like, Anthea thought, people at work do when they find out you went to an Ivy League school or drove a certain kind of car.

"We car pool together during the day."

"Oh. She has two jobs?"

"Apparently. I didn't know about this one until now." And how, she asked herself, have you spent two hours a day with someone for months on end and not known? She had looked exhausted, but Anthea had never asked her why.

"Oh."

To fill the awkward pause Anthea said, "Do you read a lot of mysteries?"

"No, just all the lesbian stuff I can." Anthea saw the couple at the next table glance at each other with slight rolls of their eyes. She suddenly realized by sitting with Paula she was announcing to everyone in the place that she was a lesbian. And Shay knew. It felt weird. Her stomach seized up into a knot of fear — it didn't know it was the Gay Nineties. Anthea mentally sighed.

Shay chose that moment to deliver the garlic bread. Anthea craved a cigarette to handle the jitters in her stomach, but instead she blurted out, "Can you sit down for a few minutes?" Paula looked at her as if she'd gone mad.

Shay glanced at Paula then said, "It's probably not a good idea."

Anthea said, "I feel horribly insensitive."

Shay said, meeting Anthea's eyes, "We just never seem to talk about the rest of our lives."

Paula said, "You mean you two didn't know the other was a dyke?" She looked Shay calmly up and down, then glanced back at Anthea. "How did you miss it?"

Shay gave Paula an unsmiling look, then turned back to Anthea. "Maybe we can develop a code in the future. Something to add to food and books." She gave a hint of a smile and zipped over to a table that was emptying. Anthea watched her move and marveled that Shay could even speak in the mornings.

"What would you need code for?" Paula finished her second slice of garlic bread and licked her fingers. I'll bet, Anthea thought, she doesn't have to exercise to keep that waistline.

"Well, we're both pretty private people. We don't talk about our home lives much."

"What are you afraid of? It's not like it's a crime to talk about it."

Paula sounded just like Lois. Anthea believed that it was no one's business. Lois had come out, or so she had claimed, with no repercussions. Except Lois hadn't been promoted in a while. Anthea realized that she hadn't been promoted anywhere in years either, and no one knew she was a lesbian. "I don't know," Anthea said. "Getting fired, I suppose, and not knowing that was the reason."

"Yeah, that could happen, and who's got the money to sue? And I don't know anybody who can afford to be out of work. Makes it hard."

I could afford it, Anthea almost said. Her parents' life and mortgage insurance had made their house all Anthea's, free of monthly payments, and left her with no financial worries at all. The sudden change in her financial status after her parents' deaths had added to her confused feelings about them. When it came right down to it, she really didn't have to work at all. They had made her childhood and adolescence pure hell. They had also given her freedom from material worries. She wanted a cigarette.

Shay delivered the pizza, chopped it into slices, dished two out onto their plates and asked if they'd like anything more. The entire process made Anthea feel very awkward. She watched Shay move on to the next table to take an order, and overheard her telling them, when they asked what she usually had, that she couldn't stand the sight of pizza anymore. Shay had a nice laugh.

She let Paula chatter on about politics and rallies she'd been to. The pizza was good, just how she liked it — not too much sauce and lots of cheese. When Shay brought the bill, Paula seized it, saying she was paying. Again, Shay gave Anthea a wink, and again, Anthea blushed. It was plain what Shay thought was going on. Anthea had no idea what was happening. She'd been in shock since they'd sat down. It was just as well Paula was paying because then it was Paula's money that covered the tip. Anthea would have felt very strange if she'd been tipping Shay. The whole situation was awkward.

They wandered slowly down Shattuck to the car. As they dodged roving bands of college students and an assortment of street people, it became easier to walk close together. Paula put her arm around Anthea's waist as they ran for a light. When they reached Anthea's car, Paula mentioned having to catch a bus. Anthea then felt compelled, since Paula had paid for her dinner, to offer Paula a ride home. It wasn't until they were actually in the car that she realized she had probably offered more than that.

"Why don't we drive up behind the Claremont? It's so bleak with most of the trees gone, but the view of the city should be terrific tonight," Paula said. "There's no moon and no fog."

"Sounds nice." She didn't mention that they would only be a few blocks from her house. She was relieved to have gained some time. Paula was very attractive. In fact, Anthea was not at all adverse to sex — she didn't owe anybody but herself explanations. Still, Paula was treating her a little bit like a slot machine. When she'd still been dating men in college, she had hated their pat assumption that if they bought dinner they got sex. But Paula had been wonderfully frank about it and maybe that made the difference.

She had the car all the way down into low gear when they finally crested a hill far above the Claremont district. A vista area had been cleared between the road and the cliffside and a dozen cars were already stopped, all facing out over the panorama of the entire Bay Area. At one end someone was taking pictures, but everyone else was in their cars, hidden from view by the darkness. A sharp wind whistled around the car when Anthea turned the engine off.

"Absolutely incredible," she heard Paula breathe. "You can see the Transamerica Tower outline."

"Do you think that's Candlestick Park?" Anthea pointed to a bright glow of lights across the dark area of water far to the south.

"No, you couldn't see it from here. You can see the Oakland Coliseum, though."

"Where?"

Paula leaned across Anthea, pointing and describing until Anthea said she could see it. Then

91

Paula turned to look at Anthea, their faces only a few inches apart. All of Anthea's hesitation faded. She hadn't felt a jolt of passion like this in ages. Since before Lois's first affair. Paula must have seen it in her eyes, because she leaned forward, gently pressing her lips to Anthea's.

"Mmm," she said. "Very nice." She kissed Anthea again, this time a little harder. Anthea relaxed back into her seat. Somewhere along the way she found her arms around Paula. Paula's hands swept over her breasts, then her stomach and Anthea arched into Paula's embrace.

"You don't hold anything back, do you?" Paula's hands returned to Anthea's breasts, recreating the same arching reaction. Anthea suddenly felt as if she were doing this too easily, but it felt so good. "I like it," Paula said. Her fingers went to the buttons of Anthea's blouse. Two were open before Anthea found her voice.

"Why don't we go to my house? It's not too far."

"Move the seat back," Paula said.

"Uh, I'd prefer more privacy," Anthea managed to say.

"We'll leave in a minute, but I can't wait to touch you. Move the seat back." Paula's voice was husky. Her lips nuzzled at Anthea's throat. Anthea found the button and the seat slowly slid backward.

What am I doing, she thought, as she pushed the button to make sure the doors were locked.

Paula straddled her and finished unbuttoning her blouse. Her fingers slipped inside and Anthea shuddered, her skin turning to gooseflesh. "Why don't you put the seat down a little?" Anthea hesitated. "We aren't doing anything wrong, you know."

She found the control and the seat reclined backward until Paula had enough room to bend... Anthea shuddered as Paula opened her blouse completely and kissed the exposed parts of Anthea's breasts.

Anthea didn't resist when Paula stripped her of her blouse and bra. Her head was whirling, her legs trembling. She realized Paula's crotch was grinding down on her own — she arched up to meet it and was delighted to hear Paula moan.

And then she fell back to the seat, and Paula's lips caressed her shoulders, then lower, across the plane of her chest. She stretched and encouraged Paula to taste her further. No, she wasn't holding anything back. In a very small part of her mind, she was writing headlines like WOMEN ARRESTED NAKED IN CAR and LESBIANS PLUNGE OVER CLIFF WHILE HAVING SEX. She grappled at the emergency brake — it was set. Then she didn't care anymore.

Paula's mouth at her breasts — the fierce and passionate movements of lips and tongue made Anthea long for that same attention between her legs. The thought of it sent pins of desire through her. She put her hand on the seam at Paula's crotch and heard Paula moan again.

"Should we go back to my place?" Anthea gasped.

"No, no," Paula said. "Let's do it here. I'm so hot for you."

Hot, yes. Anthea knew she was, too. But Paula wasn't hot for her, just hot. She was not mistaking this encounter for more than it was. Anthea admitted to herself that she was in the same condition. She wanted to have sex. And like this — well, Lois could go to hell with her accusations that Anthea had been boring. Lois should have tried this. A new surge of passion and a sense of delight filled her. As her hands went to Paula's shirt, slowly pulling it out of her pants, she felt as if she were slipping out of a cocoon.

"No," Paula murmured. "You don't have to do that. Just... put the seat down the whole way. Oh, yes, that's better."

Her mouth returned to Anthea's breasts. Anthea felt hands at her waist, then on her skirt, pulling it up. She raised her hips to make it easier. Paula moved back into the passenger seat, leaned toward Anthea, and slowly peeled Anthea's pantyhose downward.

Anthea couldn't wait. She shoved them down, baring herself in a frenzy, then opening her legs, inviting, offering. She felt her heart beating in her fingertips. Every prickle of nerves reverberated through her body and she realized she had never felt so alive before. It had never felt like this, not even her first time with a woman.

She thought, when Paula's mouth found her, she would faint.

She didn't.

She made noises she'd forgotten she knew how to make. Invoked deities and the heavens. When she was almost certain she would die of pleasure, she orgasmed.

Paula collapsed back into the passenger seat. "Oh, wow," she said.

"I'm sorry, I usually don't, I mean, not like that...."

Paula made a pleased sort of noise and said quietly, "I don't usually ... uh, dive in like that. I ... would you do something for me?"

"I could hardly refuse, could I?" Anthea leaned over to Paula, and kissed her, smelling herself on Paula's face.

"Take me to your place."

Monday morning Anthea viewed Shay's bleary eyes with compassion. She had thought Shay was just not a morning person, but now she knew better. Anthea wished there was a way she could help. And, despite Shay's obvious fatigue, she didn't miss the wink Shay gave her as she buckled up in the passenger seat. Anthea had spent a great deal of time after Paula had left wondering how she would explain Paula to Shay.

After they had pulled out into traffic, Shay fixed Anthea with an I-know-what-you've-been-up-to smiling stare.

"What?" Anthea feigned innocence and ignorance.

"I see. Pretty darned fantastic then."

"What?"

Shay grinned. "That Porsche I saw you test-driving on Friday night."

"Porsche? Oh." Anthea could feel a tiny flush

sprinkle over her cheeks. "We're talking code. I see. Well, she was more like a Ferrari."

"Four on the floor and overdrive?"

Anthea swerved to avoid a BMW that pulled out in front of her. "There were only two. On the floor. And plenty of overdrive."

"That's sickening," Shay said. "I'd be envious —" A sudden yawn overtook her. "But I don't have the energy."

"What's your schedule?"

"Whenever I get there until eleven weeknights. One to midnight on Saturdays," Shay said. Anthea reflected that she was in bed and asleep by eleven.

"Don't take this the wrong way, but I'd be happy to loan you some money."

"That's not necessary," Shay said, her voice tight and clipped.

"Oh, dear." Anthea bit her lower lip. "I've offended you. I'm sorry."

"It's all right. It's just — I've worked so hard and I guess I'd like to look back and know that I really did do it on my own. I've only got another two months of payments to the hospital and funeral home."

God, Anthea thought. To be working so hard to pay for . . . death. She felt a surge of mental virtue for having skipped her cigarette this morning. Paula didn't like cigarettes either and somehow there hadn't been time for a cigarette until Paula left late on Saturday morning. It was the first time she hadn't had a smoke after sex. She'd felt so good, she hadn't really wanted one. Maybe lots of sex was a cure for nicotine addiction. Lots of sex was probably good exercise, too. After a swallow she said, "Is there some way I can help you and not compromise your ideals?"

"No, really. I'll survive," Shay said.

"I know you will," Anthea said. "Women always do." Shay smiled slightly. "So you get Sunday off?"

"I think Sundays are a slice of heaven. I have just enough time to go to the grocery store, make up something to take for lunch during the week, laundry, and read for a couple of hours. I sleep a lot on Sundays. Or listen to tapes. I haven't bought any new music in ages, though."

"You would be very, very stupid not to let me loan you some tapes."

"My daddy didn't raise no stupid girl. I'd love to borrow anything." Shay smiled and was caught unexpectedly by a yawn that left tears in her eyes. "Jeez, excuse me. I'll wake up in about two hours. My tapes are getting so worn I can't listen to them in the Walkman when I go for a run."

"How do you find energy to go running?" Now Anthea knew where Shay got those rock-hard calves.

"I haven't lately. I'm getting out of shape for it. I used to run the four-forty in high school. And I was damned good with a javelin considering my height."

Anthea had a sudden vision of Shay, in running shorts and a tank top, gathering herself for the short run, then leaping, arm extending gracefully, her body arching with the force of her throw. Surprised, she felt a surge of something...feelings she didn't want to name. Feelings she thought Paula would have drained for quite some time to come. Just remembering how...abandoned she'd been made her tingle.

Anthea turned up the traffic report and only

after it was over did she feel courageous enough to say, "Don't you think it's long odds that we are both lesbians and ended up in the same car pool?"

Shay didn't answer, so Anthea glanced over. She was asleep. Anthea sighed. It had seemed like a big step to actually say the L-word to Shay. Just to make sure there was no misunderstanding. Just to be sure that Shay knew she wasn't bisexual or just curious or desperate or something.

She let her sleep.

5
Acceleration

Shay managed a mumbled greeting and a muttered remark about the cold wind. Anthea pressed the control to increase the heat in the car, even though she told herself it was absurd to have to. It was June, for heaven's sake. *Ah well.*

"Welcome to summer in the Bay Area," she said aloud. "The tourists are arriving and the fog has come in just for them. Did you have a good night?"

Shay glared at Anthea for a moment, then said

in a low, threatening tone, "Anthea, I'm warning you, perk down or else."

"I see," Anthea said. "Not a good night at all."

"Let's just say that if I ever see a pizza again, I'll throw up."

Shay seemed more human once they were headed south on 880. She dozed for a while, then sat up, seemingly more alert. Anthea said, "You know, considering the way you feel about pizza, I'm surprised you want free pepperoni."

"I give it to my upstairs neighbor, Mrs. Giordano. The name says it all."

"What does she do with it?"

"She makes pizza and other delectable concoctions on Sundays. All day Sunday. If you want something to eat, you just drop in. No questions asked, no need to pay her. She must be keeping twenty or thirty old people in the HUD project down the street alive with her Sunday meals."

Anthea thought about her huge savings account balance. Her paid-for house. Her paid-for car. Mrs. Giordano filling people's plates all day Sunday. "What a wonderful thing," she said softly.

"I used to help her, but lately she won't let me. She says a nice Japanese girl like me doesn't know how to make pizza anyway. I keep telling her I'm a fourth-generation American, but she just shakes her head. She came to this country about thirty years ago and says she'll always be Italian and I'll always be Japanese and that is what being an American means." Shay laughed fondly. "Sometimes she mixes the leftover pizza sauce into spaghetti sauce and we have it over noodles I make. She says Japanese girls make good noodles because we invented them." Shay laughed again. "I keep telling her that the Chinese invented noodles. She's a very sweet lady. She knows I'm religiously unaffiliated, so she keeps hoping I'll become a Catholic. She's amazing — she's even been encouraging me to, uh, test drive."

Anthea choked back a giggle. "Girl cars?"

"Girl cars. She wants me to find the right girl car and settle down. She's convinced settling down is the best thing to do with your life."

Anthea recalled her dreams of settling down with Lois. She had thought they were settled down, but it hadn't worked out that way. Out of the corner of her eye, Anthea watched Shay's hands draw little curls and smooth planes in the air as she described the latest book she was reading. She felt relaxed, then caught herself casually reaching toward the pocket she used to keep cigarettes in. Damn . . . just when she thought she'd kicked it, she'd find herself reaching for them again. She caught herself tapping the bottom of packs of gum like they were cigarette lighters.

"— so I really recommend it."

Anthea realized that she hadn't been paying attention to what Shay was saying, only the movement of her hands. "I thought you said English was your least favorite subject."

"It was in school. I read a lot now. I read to my father when he was in the hospital — mostly geologic journals, but sometimes a book I thought he'd like."

"It doesn't matter where you learned to appreciate books, as long as you do. That's what Mrs. Pritchard always said."

"Who's Mrs. Prichard?"

"My tenth-grade English teacher." My first crush,

Anthea added to herself, heaving a big sigh. Why she hadn't figured out she was a lesbian until college, she didn't know, but Anthea would never forget Emily Dickinson on the lips of Mrs. Pritchard.

"I see," Shay said. "Sure she wasn't the gym teacher?"

"No," Anthea said. "But she should have been."

Shay grinned. "I had several gym teachers in college, and a whole bunch in graduate school."

"Where'd you go to graduate school?"

"The Missouri School of Mines. It's the Harvard of geology schools."

"Would it be stereotypical for me to assume that there's lots of test drivers there?"

"No more than average," Shay said. Her shoulders were shaking with laughter. "But I think I drove with them all. Turned out to be a good thing because it's been a long, long time since I've, uh, hit the road."

"You drove with all of them? One at a time, or. . . ."

"One at a time, of course," Shay said, with feigned indignation. "I didn't do . . . car pools." She and Anthea waved cheerily at the guard.

"Didn't that waste energy?" Anthea pushed their parking lot card into the reader, then drove forward toward their space.

"Yes, yes it did. It was before my own personal energy crisis."

Anthea turned the engine off and looked at Shay. They burst into laughter. After a few moments, Anthea managed to say, "We could write a comic strip. How to categorize lesbians by the type of car they represent."

"I'd be a horse and buggy."

Anthea didn't agree, but she kept her opinion back. She headed for her shuttle stop after a wave. Shay was definitely a sports car, but Anthea didn't know yet what kind. She quelled the thought that there was only one way to find out. She was not going to get involved with another woman she car pooled with.

On Shay's desk, new data awaited. She took it to the copy room and made herself two sets. She liked to pencil in codes and notes on the sheets without messing up the original. She filed one copy as a spare, clipped the original to her cube wall where she could glance at it, and then began going over the working copy.

"This can't be right," Shay said to herself. *I really must be groggy not to have noticed sooner.* That or still in a daze about how Anthea's cheeks got flushed when she laughed. *Stop that this instant!*

Harold grunted. "What can't be right?"

"This soil analysis result. The xylene is practically off the scale. There's no xylene being manufactured near there. This is impossible. Oh shit, do you believe this? These aren't my results. They aren't even NOC-U's results. They're for NEM, Inc., whatever that is. How could the lab make a mistake like this?"

"Because I'll bet you they were low bidder," Harold said. "Go complain to Scott."

Shay did. Scott took the printout array back and promised to locate the real results. Shay offered to call the lab herself, but Scott said he'd handle it. Really kick butt over it.

She had just gotten her next project underway when he arrived with another printout, this time plainly labeled for NOC-U.

"Thanks, I'll get started, then," Shay said, already calling up the macro to relaunch the array of spreadsheets she needed. She glanced at the result for well B-B-146. "This is much better, but it's still too high."

"Which one," Scott said.

"B-B-one-four-six. I knew it wasn't above hazard, but I still didn't think it was approaching the line." Shay stopped, shook her head. Some piece of data was out of place. She concentrated for a moment, but whatever inconsistency bothered her refused to surface. She went on, "If I remember right, it's up a ways from last quarter." Shay pulled a file from her drawer.

"That must be the sample spike," Scott said.

"Not that one. I took it myself. One-four-seven was a spike. One-four-six is a watch well. It would be foolish to spike the sample."

"Maybe there was a mix-up," Scott suggested. "It doesn't seem likely that a well sample would jump in parts per billion like that in one quarter."

"I could do a curve over the last two years," Shay said. "See if there's a pattern. Contrast it to rainfall."

"Oh, no, that won't be necessary. I'm sure it's an error of some sort."

"This is a bona fide hot spot," Shay said, her temper getting shorter. There had been nothing wrong with her sample, and it had not been deliberately spiked to test the lab's accuracy. "See, here are the three sampling spikes, and the three blanks. There's a lot of groundwater movement in that area. That could explain the higher concentrations. And we had a lot of rain last quarter, increasing the water movement."

"But the bay mud provides a permeability barrier in that part of the refinery."

"But there's a saline difference. The density between A and C zone mud has to be corrected for salinity. The velocity head isn't going to factor in here, but when two aquifers have waters of different density, the total head is affected." Shay stopped short. Scott was staring at her.

"I'll ask the chemists about it," he said. "You aren't a chemist, are you?"

"No, but I know what I'm talking about."

"Well, sure. I tell you what. You go ahead on the basis of these results and write up the tables for the quarterly report. Meanwhile, I'll check the samples and your questions. Maybe there's another explanation. I think we've underestimated you, Sumoto." He left after another sharp look at her.

Shay felt a glow, glad to have finally had a chance to show that she did have practical experience and a strong theoretical background.

"Now how come you didn't tell me you knew more about groundwater geology than just about anyone on this project?" Harold pushed back from his desk and looked at her.

"You wouldn't have believed me," Shay said.

"Yes I would. Now I think they do, too. You could be sorry."

"What do you mean?"

Harold rubbed his hands over his hair. He dropped his voice. "Haven't you noticed that, present company excepted, there is a vortex of stupidity on this project?"

"Yeah, I have," Shay said with a smile. "I thought that was just private-industry standard."

"I don't think so. I think they don't want anyone too bright around here."

"That doesn't make any sense. This is really complicated data."

"But what does everyone do when there's any sort of problem? We're practically told to assume the lab made a mistake or the sample got spiked or the analysis was flawed. This is the working formula: if the soil here is not contaminated, then. . . ."

"Then the samples must be bad. But who says the soil is clean?"

"NOC-U, that's who."

Shay swallowed. "I think I forgot who signed my piddly paycheck."

"And?"

"I don't give a damn. That report is going to be accurate. We're talking about a hot spot just over a hundred yards from a direct channel to the bay. We're talking about a delicate ecosystem."

"I know. Can you afford to lose this job?"

"I can't afford to lose what's left of the San Francisco Bay," Shay said. "God, maybe it was a spike, but I don't think so. Let's wait and see what Scott finds out."

"Right," Harold said, returning to his computer. "I'm sure it'll be inspired."

Shay looked at his broad back, then, with a sigh, started entering data into her analysis spreadsheet.

Her earlier hunch that some piece of data was wrong nagged at her again, but wouldn't solidify. She pushed her misgivings aside and let her fingers fly over the keyboard. She was tired and sorely tempted not to fight about what might be a simple lab mistake.

Anthea was nervous when she got to her car; her boss was with her. Shay was approaching from the other side of the lot. She prayed that Shay wouldn't pick up their conversation of this morning where they had left off. She waved and saw Shay's eyebrows go up in puzzlement.

"Hi there," she said. "This is Martin Lawrence, my boss. He needs a lift over to Fremont. Martin, this is Shay Sumoto, my fellow car poolee."

"Just say the word if it's not convenient," Martin said.

"No problem," Shay said. "Anthea's the pilot of the day. Here, let me get in the back. I've got shorter legs than you."

Anthea felt some of her panic subside. What had she been worried about, that Shay would walk up and say, "Hello, you lesbian you. Is this your boss? Gee, you've got a great dyke working for you. She had really good sex recently with a cute young thing she'd just met."

Martin said, "My car's in the shop, and my girlfriend and I could work out the next couple of days except for me getting home tonight. You can drop me at the video store right off the freeway."

Anthea said, "I rented *Working Girl* last

weekend. I'd forgotten why I didn't want to see it. It was rather disappointing."

"I enjoyed it a lot," Martin said, his tone surprised.

"I didn't like it at all," Shay said. "It's supposed to be about women in business, but the two women just fight over a man."

"But you've got to admit Melanie Griffith is one fine-looking woman." He cast a knowing glance over his shoulder at Shay.

Anthea found that a very odd thing to say. Why would a man ask a woman if she thought another woman was attractive? Was he implying he'd guessed Shay was a lesbian? No, she thought. She was just being paranoid.

"Sigourney Weaver is more my taste," Shay said. Anthea's pulse rate went right back up. "The movie was sexist all the way through. Even the title. *Working Girl*. Melanie Griffith was most definitely a woman."

"I thought it was a play on what they call hookers," Martin said.

Anthea tried desperately to think of a way to steer the conversation to less hostile waters.

"So it was all about women being sex objects for men. Working girls." Shay seemed content to leave it at that.

Anthea glanced at her in the rear view mirror. She'd never seen this side of Shay, or Martin for that matter. Shay was staring out the window with a frown. Anthea studied the curve of Shay's cheek. She hadn't said anything Anthea disagreed with — just a lot she'd never say to her boss. Of course, she would have said she'd never let Paula do what she did in her car, but then she had. And she had liked it a lot. Ever since then she'd felt so much happier. Who knew what she was capable of? She smiled to herself. She could be capable of a great many things.

"What do they call hookers in your country?" Martin suddenly asked.

After a moment Anthea closed her mouth.

"Are you talking to me?" Shay asked incredulously.

"Of course," Martin said.

"I was born in the U.S. of A., Martin. So was my mother and her mother and the one before that. The same is true on my dad's side. One of my great-grandfathers was Norwegian."

"Oh, that's why your accent is so faint."

"I wasn't aware I had an accent," Shay said, her tone taut. "English is my first and only language. The same as it was for both my parents."

"Oh." Martin's tone was flat. "Well, it must be nice to go back to your home country. "

Anthea envisioned a paper doll Martin being put through the shredder.

Through gritted teeth Shay said, "This is my home country. And I don't visit Japan because my family hasn't lived there for a hundred and forty or so years. I only know of very, very distant relatives. Aside from a bit of DNA and a last name, I have nothing in common with them."

"Oh, what a shame. I always thought it would be nice to have an ancient heritage."

Anthea opened and closed her mouth but no sound came out.

"I am an American of Japanese ancestry. And I have a dash of that highly valued Northern European blood. I do have an ancient heritage."

"But if you are just American —"

"I've never thought of myself as *just* an American," Shay said, primly. "I'd rather be an American than any other nationality on the planet."

"Well, of course," Martin said. "Anyone would."

Anthea saw Shay smile, but it had a dangerous edge.

"But don't you want to see Japan?" Martin asked, his tone tinged with sarcasm. "Meet a nice Japanese boy?"

Anthea realized that Martin had figured out, in less than three minutes, that Shay was a lesbian. It had taken her three months. *That makes me stupid, but what does it make him?*

"I'm not a nice Japanese girl," Shay said. "Not all Japanese girls like Japanese boys."

Anthea felt stabbing pains in her chest. It was either hysteria or a heart attack. Either one would provide a good diversion, she thought desperately. Fortunately, a bus cut her off at that moment and Anthea had to slam on the brakes. Martin almost went through the windshield. He began holding forth on how the mass transit systems in the Bay Area could be improved, and Anthea glanced back at Shay. There were two spots of bronze color in her cheeks as she glared at the back of Martin's head. Anthea wanted to push Martin out the door into the path of the nearest mass transit vehicle.

They dropped him at a shopping center just off the freeway in Fremont, and Shay transferred to the passenger seat. Anthea lost no time putting as much distance between Shay and Martin as possible.

"Cover your ears," Shay said when they stopped at a light.

"Why?"

"Just do it."

Anthea covered her ears and still plainly heard Shay's scream, a mixture of anger and exasperation.

"Okay, I'm through."

"I've done that myself on more than one occasion," Anthea said. She was wondering if Shay sounded like that during — "I don't know what it is about him, but I can't wait for the day he's promoted. He's so . . . stupid!"

Shay shook her head. "This is unbelievable. Don't they give managers any sort of sensitivity training?"

Anthea shrugged. "It's mandatory but only a few hours every two years. Obviously, it isn't sinking in."

"You'd have thought I was the kitchen help . . . the kind of person you can say anything to because they can't talk back."

"I'm sorry," Anthea said.

"It's not your fault. You can't control the man's arrogance. You have no idea how many times in my life I've been complimented on my command of English." She stared out the window while her hands twisted and flexed in her lap.

"I really want his job." Anthea didn't know what else to say. She felt horribly guilty for having exposed Shay to Martin's racist comments.

"If there's anything I can do to help you get it, just say the word."

They spent the remainder of the drive mainly in

silence. Anthea brooded later about how different the drive home had been from the drive to work. She hoped Shay wouldn't hold Martin's crass racism against her. And though Shay had hardly needed it, she chided herself for not having come to Shay's defense.

Shay slid out of the car quietly when they reached Luciano's. She was seething with undiluted rage, but if she vented a little she'd let it all out on Anthea when what she really wanted was to hit Martin, hit him very hard. She wanted to shove a photograph under his nose, the one of her father at the age of 2, picking flowers. It had been taken by a government official, who had claimed it proved Japanese families were happy in their internment camps.

She wasn't paying attention to her footing as she murmured a halfhearted goodnight to Anthea and suddenly, she was on her hands and knees, shaking her head. She sat back, making sure which way was up first. She rubbed the door of Anthea's car where her head had hit it. Fortunately, neither the door nor her head seemed dented. Stars danced before her for a moment, then an arm circled her shoulders.

"Are you okay?"

"Yes," Shay said. She started to get to her feet and Anthea pulled her up, her arm now most firmly around Shay's waist. All the anger she was directing at Martin fused into heat and the heat turned to Anthea. She wanted to ask Anthea if she thought of her as Japanese or American or foreign or a friend?

Did she think of Shay as a woman — the way that Shay knew she was beginning to think of Anthea? Their bodies were so close, and Shay felt seared and confused by flaming desire. She trembled violently.

"You aren't okay." It was a statement.

"No, really, I'm fine. Just shook up." She stepped away from Anthea. It felt as if she left her skin behind. She brushed at the knees of her slacks. "I'm lucky I didn't rip these pants. They're my favorites." She looked up at Anthea.

"You're sure you're okay?"

Shay lied. "I'm fine."

Her head had a small bump Shay didn't tell Anthea about, but it didn't cause the incessant headache she had for the next three days. The headache started when she decided to ignore Scott's instructions and work on an idea for remediation of the xylene.

She plugged in data that correlated rainfall, her estimate of the groundwater velocity — based on the permeability of the clayey soil — and the increase in xylene at well B-B-146. With a spate of research into the refinery maps, she plotted the direction of the water movement. Much to her surprise, however, she wasn't able to determine a source of the xylene leak. The xylene process wasn't on this side of the refinery. There shouldn't be xylene there at all, but there was and had been for the last two years. And it was increasing. She set aside for now the fact that she couldn't determine the source. It was a mystery she would eventually solve.

Her mind was already grappling with the remediation possibilities. How could they remove the xylene and leave the soil and water table intact? At the rate of movement there was as much as seven years' grace before the flow reached the open water channel that led to the San Francisco Bay. Plenty of time for a relatively inexpensive and thorough remediation. A 200-foot channel with forced pumping of groundwater through a bioreactor might work. And it would screen out other substances which, while not hazardous, wouldn't do the marine life any good.

She went back to her report and wrote up the suggested remediation, including her estimates and plot of the water movement. She worked through lunch, munching distractedly on her peanut butter and jelly sandwich. When she finally copied her report to a floppy disk to take to word processing for formatting, she realized she didn't remember eating her sandwich at all. She was exhausted and considered long and hard calling in sick at the pizza parlor. The thought was appealing, but when she finally quit she would get her sick leave in pay. She was counting on it as a little nest egg so she could quit a bit sooner. She couldn't afford to miss a day.

She credited her exhaustion with the fact that she spent the entire drive home — without the presence of any racist S.O.B.s from the refinery — excruciatingly aware that she wanted to put her head down in Anthea's lap and go to sleep. Since sleep occurred to her before anything else she might do with her head in Anthea's lap, she knew she was tired. Too tired to fight the breathless ache she felt as she examined Anthea's shapely calves, caressed by taupe hose. They were the epitome of femininity. The epitome of the kind of calves that normally did not attract her. She wondered why she had only admired muscled, taut calves before. She wondered when she would get a full night's sleep.

She wondered if this was what it felt like to be on the edge of a breakdown. She let her gaze travel up the back of Anthea's calves to the soft area behind her knees. She got a warm glow in her stomach and then felt as if she'd just eaten a couple of chocolate bars. If this was a mental breakdown, she could live with it.

"Takes all kinds," Martin said.

His sudden appearance startled Anthea. She turned to face him as he leaned nonchalantly against her cube wall. She shook her head. "Come again?"

"Your car pool mate. A real militant, isn't she?"

"No, not really. I think you brought out her ... opinions."

"Well, you're certainly tolerant. Beggars can't be choosers, I suppose."

Anthea started to speak, but she was stopped by a wave of nausea, followed by a hot flash and cold sweat. "I'm more ..." she stuttered. "I'm. ..." Her phone rang.

She answered in a shaken voice, then began rattling off the cost data for yet another anxious product manager. Martin gave a wave and disappeared in the direction of his office. When Anthea finished her call she couldn't recall what column of data she had read. She hoped it was the right one or the no-brand all-purpose oil profit estimates would be in sorry shape.

She took a deep breath. She had almost said it. Almost. But lord, who would have thought mere words really could stick in your throat? For a moment she had thought she was going to be sick. Over saying a few words!

What was she thinking of . . . she knew that coming out at work would cost her any hope of Martin's job. Not that she'd be able to prove discrimination. What was motivating her to give it up? Nothing had changed. A tiny voice reminded her that something was different — her body still felt the imprint of Shay's. Her arms tingled from being around Shay. It had only been for a moment, but she had felt electrified. She didn't want to feel this way. She was just going to get hurt again.

She shivered and fought down the queasy roil in her stomach and gradually the sounds around her invaded again. Over the hum of air-conditioning and her hard drive she could hear Adrian on the phone, speaking in an unusually low voice. Anthea had learned that when Adrian was quiet on the phone, he usually needed to talk afterward — if only to exult over a date with a new guy or a weekend trip to wine country for the sunshine.

His voice rose slightly and she could make out the words. "I thought he was stable . . . shit. Oh shit." Adrian's words took on a breathy, choked quality. "He loves that car — always joked that he wanted to be buried in it. I know, I know, that was before this, but . . . okay. I'll ask around. I'd buy it myself if I could, but I couldn't pay him what it's worth, and certainly not in time."

After Adrian had hung up, Anthea could tell he was sitting very still. She picked up the thickest report she could find and a pencil, then assumed an air of nonchalance. She sat down next to his desk, not looking at him yet, and opened the report. She let lots of green and white striped computer paper ruffle to the ground. No one — particularly Martin — would come within a mile. Adrian finally said, "What the hell are you doing?"

"Faking it. So what's new?"

Adrian sat back in his chair, eyes closed. "Goddam paper-thin walls."

"They're not walls in case you hadn't noticed. Can I help?"

"It's not likely." He rubbed his eyes vigorously, then put his glasses back on. He looked at Anthea owlishly, hiding behind the lenses. "Not unless you want to buy a sixty-nine mint-condition fire-engine red VW bug ragtop last appraised at ten thousand. A friend is running out of time and needs all the money he can get for the duration — rent, AZT, food. Christ, he cleaned that car with a diaper and a baby's toothbrush. Rebuilt every piece of the engine himself."

Anthea could feel her heart accelerating. How many times? This would make five, she thought. Five of Adrian's friends had "run out of time," as he always put it. He was too young to have a suit specifically set aside for funerals. She felt helpless and selfish, and everything Lois had ever said about her started to replay in her head. She said, in a faint voice, "I'll give him twelve thousand for it."

"Don't kid around, Andy," Adrian said.

"I'm not kidding. I can write a check."

"You never told me you were rich." He obviously still thought she was joking.

"I have no house payment. I don't spend much on clothes. I'm satisfied with a mere five pairs of shoes. I clean my own house. I have no dependents. And God knows no one to travel with and I hate traveling alone. I only buy new things when old things break." Anthea shrugged. She felt numb all over suddenly. "It's only money. Lois said that giving away money was all I was good for and I suppose —"

"Now we're getting at the truth," Adrian said. "Lois was a bitch and that's no reason to buy a car you don't need."

"I know that. It won't even dent my money market balance."

"Don't you even have it invested in something with a better return?"

"It seems greedy when I already have enough. Besides, rates aren't what they used to be. My parents believed in lots and lots of life insurance." She shrugged again.

Adrian shook his head. "I think you need to spend a little of that nest egg on more therapy, my dear."

"I suppose so. Except I can tell you word for word exactly what a therapist will say and then what I'll say. So why bother? It would be a waste of money." At that she laughed. "I don't make any sense sometimes, least of all to me."

"I noticed. I have no idea why you even work here."

"It's what I went to school for. I really went to

school to escape my parents, but the official story was I wanted to get my MBA."

"That makes no sense whatsoever."

"Yes, it does. I'm not ready to admit I spent six years in college and God knows how much money just to get away from my parents. Besides, coming to work every day is something to do —"

"And you do it well." He stared at her as if he was only seeing her for the first time. "I'd go nuts if you went anywhere else. Tell you what." Adrian reached over and patted her on the head. "Let Uncle Adrian have all your money and he'll give you an allowance."

"I'm not that stupid," Anthea said. As the numb feeling faded she realized that it was how she used to feel all the time, ever since Lois's first affair. "I'm serious about the car. I —" She stopped, about to say that she thought Shay would be totally shocked and pleased when she saw it. Shay had nothing to do with this. "I've always wanted something a little more outrageous. I would really like to have it and I'd take very good care of it. And . . . and you can tell your friend that if he ever wants to buy it back, it's his."

Adrian's mocking expression disappeared. "He's only got six months, maybe more, and it's the car or move into a group home. His savings are long gone and he just got an eviction notice. I thought he had worked everything out with his family, but apparently they've faded away now that the really hard times have arrived." His Adam's apple bobbed. "Are you sure? Really sure?"

Anthea dumped the rest of the report on the

floor and went back to her cubicle. She came back with a checkbook. "Who do I make it out to?"

"You haven't even seen the car!"

Anthea smiled archly. "If it's not as you said it was, I'll have you dropped in the oxidation ponds. You'd glow in the dark for the rest of your days."

Adrian smirked. "Now that's a new thought. You wouldn't need a glow-in-the-dark condom if you had a glow-in-the-dark body."

Anthea gaped and blushed. "Please, my tender years," she managed to say. She waved the checkbook at him. "Name, please."

Adrian took a deep breath and then a tremulous smile lit his face. "You're a prince. And darling, you are going to look magnificent in that car."

Shay thought Anthea looked excited about something. Her eyes were sparkling. Maybe another date with the Ferrari. The thought gave Shay a twinge of envy. "Another test drive," she asked as she merged over from the 280 lanes to 880.

"As a matter of fact," Anthea said, "yes." Suddenly she gave Shay a blinding flashbulb smile. "This time it's a fire-engine red Volkswagen bug. A convertible."

Shay blinked. Convertible? Did she mean bisexual? She glanced at Anthea when she could. She opened her mouth to ask outright, then hesitated. Anthea looked as if she was going to have hysterics — her face was flushed pink. Even her hair seemed to sparkle. She had never seen her so animated. The difference made her wonder what

Anthea looked like when she... Shay stomped on the thought. Fire-engine red? Did that mean a fire fighter? A bisexual fire fighter?

"Mint condition."

A young, bisexual fire fighter. "Right." Shay was at a loss for words.

"I'm picking it up on Sunday. Probably test drive all over the city."

"There's no need to gloat," Shay said. A young, bisexual fire fighter with stamina. Fine, she thought. I have an open mind.

"Well, it's not every day something as cute and sassy comes along. In such good shape."

Jeeez Laweez. She didn't have to go on about it. Shay was already green with envy. And she hadn't thought Anthea would be so fixated on looks. "Well," she said, "appearance isn't everything."

"Oh, of course not," Anthea said. "Performance is what matters. It's a classic. A sixty-nine model." Anthea had a fit of giggles. Shay hadn't thought Anthea knew how. Lately she'd been more prone to giggling. Ever since she'd been in the pizza parlor with that baby butch.

It had been a surprise to find out Anthea was a lesbian — she just didn't look the part to Shay. She supposed Anthea could be bisexual. Maybe the baby butch had been Anthea's moment of conversion. That was a depressing thought. But ever since she'd realized that Anthea was a lesbian, Shay had found it harder and harder to not think about her.

"Don't be crude," Shay said, wondering what Anthea would look like with her hair loose. The thought of it in her hands made her body twinge. She was shocked by the way she wanted to touch

Anthea's hair, and every other place. Maybe she was jealous of the baby butch for being the one who showed Anthea the light. She told herself that she needed to get out there and do some test driving of her own. Sure, she had plenty of time to try and find a date. She could look between three and five p.m. every Sunday.

"Adrian says it really performs," Anthea said, wiping her eyes.

Shay knew Adrian was Anthea's closest work buddy. She gave herself the time it took to change over two lanes. Then she said, "Have I missed something?"

"The part about the car," Anthea said. "That I just bought."

Shay laughed so hard she changed lanes without meaning to. Finally, she said, "If you have money to burn what are you working for?"

"Because I need to and I want to."

"Well, sure," Shay said. "But why on earth NOC-U? For next to nothing? A place were it takes three days to get a lousy report formatted and printed out?"

"It's the job I've always had," Anthea said. "I got it after my MBA."

"But . . . Oh, great. An accident." Shay let the car drift to a stop. They inched along as everyone ahead of them took a good, long look at two cars stopped in the median strip. "You'd think they've never seen two cars by the side of the road before." She shot a worried glance at her thermometer gauge. This kind of traffic was hard on her car. And it felt like the hottest day of the summer. Tomorrow would be freezing fog, no doubt. It wouldn't be this warm again until October.

Anthea rolled down her window and slipped out of her suit jacket. Shay realized she couldn't take her gaze off of Anthea's blouse. When she finally tore her attention back to the road, the sight of those soft, full swells under a high-collared silk shirt was burned in her mind's eye like the afterglow of an acetylene torch. Good God, she thought. It had been too long. They were probably as soft as mounds of Mrs. Giordano's baby tushy pizza dough. Shay trembled and realized she was salivating, which revolted her enough that she could breathe again. She was not salivating over Anthea. Absolutely not. Anthea was definitely not her type . . . closeted, apparently rich, and . . . well, not athletic. Even if her calves were fabulous. Think about groundwater remediation, she told herself. Think about your report to the Water Board. Think of a white bear.

The traffic stayed thick all the way into Oakland. Finally, they left the freeway on Ashby and took surface streets into Berkeley. Almost ninety minutes from the time they had left the refinery, Shay pulled up alongside Anthea's car where she had left it on Hearst. "What will you do with this car now that you're bringing home a cute, sassy VW? It'll probably get jealous."

Anthea arched her eyebrows. "I think there's room enough in my life to drive two cars."

"My, my," Shay said. "You *are* adventurous." Maybe there was room in her life for two women. Stop that! My God, Shay thought. What was happening here?

"Oh stop," Anthea said. "Actually, I feel quite decadent. I'll have to make good use of both of them and make them last the rest of my life. One for commuting and one for fun."

"A convertible," Shay said with a sigh. "I've always wanted a convertible."

"Would you . . . no, Sunday's your day off."

"What?"

"I was wondering if you'd like to come with me to pick it up? You'd be doing me a favor," Anthea said. "Adrian was going to follow me home in my car and I was going to drive him home again which was going to take an incredible amount of time. This way you could follow me and I'll drop you back. I'd even . . . buy dinner. I was going to take Adrian and his friend — the guy who's selling me the car — out to someplace they like."

"Well," Shay said. *You shouldn't, you know you shouldn't. It would take up your only free day.* She needed groceries and she had books to return. She said, "I'd love to." *Oh shit.*

"I'll pick you up at two."

Anthea was gone in a ripple of silk and legs. Shay drove to her apartment parking lot in a daze. As she locked the car and then walked around the corner and up the two blocks to Luciano's, she tried to decide if Sunday was a date. No. Couldn't be. She was doing Anthea a favor. That wasn't a date. No way. Just a friendly arrangement. Right. She had given up the few hours of her precious free time for no reason at all when her brain was mired with constituent parts per billion and velocity heads. As she opened the door to Luciano's she decided it was definitely not a date. And she was a fool to think otherwise.

6
Merging Lanes

Anthea flicked through hanger after hanger. Black suit, gray suit, navy blue suit, black skirt, white blouse, white blouse, gray suit, a navy blue skirt. So much for the hope that the back of the closet would reveal something to wear. She sighed and started at the beginning again. The brighter suits in the front broke up the monotony, but one fact was very plain: she had no apparel appropriate

126

to joyriding in a cute and sassy car. Sitting next to Shay, no less. Her closet was only half full, and it was one hundred percent business clothes. Even the slacks were formal. Why on earth didn't she own a pair of jeans? Finally, she selected a pair of linen pants — basic black. *Basic boring.*

She turned to the shelves where her sweaters were stacked. Something for riding around in the sun with the top down. The sun had been shining since it had come up over the hills — unusual for summer — but the temperature wouldn't go over sixty-five. The turquoise cashmere Lois had given her caught her eye. It was lightweight and it didn't clash with her hair. She would just forget the source. Dressed, finally, she hurried out to her car and headed for Shay's.

When she got there she realized she didn't know if she should wait or if Shay would mind her going to the door. Shay was so private about some things, like about working a second job. An old woman was helping another even older woman down the stairs from the second floor. When they reached the bottom step, the two women parted company with a wave, and one headed for the street. The other woman squinted at Anthea, then waved.

Anthea got out of the car, certain she was about to meet the redoubtable Mrs. Giordano.

"You are here for Shay? She is upstairs. Oh, there you are," Mrs. Giordano said as Shay appeared at the top of the steps. "Stop wiping dishes, your date is here," she announced, waving at Shay. As Shay came down the stairs, Anthea found herself on the receiving end of an appraising stare. "You work with Shay?"

"We don't work together, but we work for the same company."

"You've been there a long time? You have the pension plan?"

"Yes," Anthea said. Mrs. Giordano was an odd inquisitor. "I'm vested one hundred percent."

"Good, good. Shay is such a nice girl," Mrs. Giordano said.

"A woman, not a girl," Shay said as she joined them.

"In my day," Mrs. Giordano began, "a woman tried to stay a girl all her life. But it's not my day anymore. Now I'm supposed to say right out I'm an old woman. Well, it's true." She gave Anthea another piercing glance. "You two have fun on your date." She turned to Shay. "Remember, you have to work tomorrow." Her eyebrows arched significantly as she gave Anthea a last look and went back up the stairs.

"I gather I'm to have you back by curfew," Anthea said with a smile.

"I told her it wasn't a date exactly. . . ."

"Not exactly," Anthea said. Her body abruptly goose-pimpled. She had the feeling that everything had changed. "Well, let's go."

But then again, everything seemed the same when they were in the car. Except they were headed for San Francisco and traffic was a lot lighter than usual. She pressed up a selection of CDs and they cruised into the city to the bouncing tones of the Manhattan Transfer. She handed a sheet of paper to Shay. "Tell me what Adrian wrote down."

"Where are we headed?"

"Northwest corner of Market and Noe. Adrian is meeting us there and then he'll direct us to his friend's house. The one with the car."

"Oh, take this exit," Shay said. "Noe and Market's just a block off Castro."

"I don't know where that is," Anthea admitted.

"This is your first time to the Castro?"

"Well, I was there once, but I felt . . . out of place."

Shay chewed on her lip for a few moments, then said, "Well, I'll help you streak your hair purple if you like. Or we could go shopping for leather chaps. But you don't have to go the whole nine yards all at once."

"I'm not sure I'd fit in," Anthea said. "I guess I'm a little conservative."

Shay smiled. "That'll change."

"Or maybe not." Anthea frowned. "I am what I am. I'm not flamboyant. I'm not political —"

"There are those who say, um, just having sex with another woman is political."

"I don't feel that way. It's private. It's . . . a choice I made."

Shay frowned slightly, then chewed on her lip again. "But if it's a permanent choice it's going to affect your life."

"It hasn't so far."

Shay looked out the window. "It's only been a short while. At the light drive ahead about four blocks."

"Okay. What do you mean, short while?" Anthea wished they had never started talking about politics. Lois would have been spouting the latest straight-people-are-out-to-get-us story from the *Sentinel* by now. Keeping up with each insult and thoughtless act made Anthea tired and depressed.

"Wasn't . . . um, that woman. I mean wasn't that. . . ."

Anthea blinked, then realized what Shay's line of reasoning was. She was peeved that Shay couldn't believe Anthea had been a lesbian for more than a few weeks. What was she missing, a dozen earrings and pink triangles hanging off her ears?

"No, that was not my first time. My first time was in a professor's office at the University of Chicago with a teaching assistant. Some fifteen years ago. Since then I've had enough practice to keep my skills up and I even lived with another woman."

"I'm sorry, I just, I mean I hadn't realized. . . ."

"Well, now you know." Anthea didn't know why she was so bothered. "We come in all shapes and sizes and we can't all belong to Queer Nation." There, that was why she was upset. Shay sounded just like Lois all over again.

"I know that," Shay said. "Look, I just wasn't expecting it. I had ruled you out without really thinking about it — shame on me. You don't have to join Queer Nation to prove you're a lesbian."

"One of the reasons I'm not involved in the activist agenda is that I've been discounted once too often because I'm not suffering because I'm gay. This lesbian writer was on a talk show — everyone says she's a 'thinking lesbian's lesbian' — and said that lesbian affluence was a myth. I felt like she'd slapped me. She went on and on about visibility after she'd just made me invisible. I don't need to be treated like dirt, certainly not by other lesbians."

130

Shay said quietly, "You know, I do understand where you're coming from. You haven't had any firsthand experience with oppression. It doesn't make you less gay. But have you ever tried to do anything that pushes the envelope?"

"What do you mean?"

"Well, for example, let's say you wanted to get married. But you know it's against the law. So you never try to get a license so, in a way, you haven't been deprived of a right because you never tried to use it. You're saving the government the trouble of denying you rights by denying them to yourself."

Anthea hadn't really thought of it that way. But what didn't she have that she wanted? She sighed. She decided to change the subject. "Where are we?"

Shay seemed grateful for a new topic. "Rapidly passing through a corner of the Mission district on our way to the Castro. I tried to find an apartment around here, but I couldn't afford it. I love the variety of neighborhoods. You can walk to just about any kind of deli or grocery you might desire, and there's entertainment of all kinds."

"I've always lived in Berkeley, right where I'm living now," Anthea said. "Where do I go?"

"One home all your life — turn left at the light and then we're on Market — I can't imagine it. We moved around so much. Stay in the right-hand lane."

"It feels like I moved since the fire. It was rebuilt from the foundation up."

"How awful — you lost the house you grew up in to the fire?"

Anthea swallowed. "It wasn't so bad. A lot of memories went too and that was for the best. I got to rebuild and the floor plan is much better. The old house had a lot of added on rooms. The kitchen was down the hall from the dining room, for example." She ignored Shay's searching glance and went on blithely, "My parents were always intending to remodel but they never got around to it."

"We always rented. Some places we lived were fairly primitive, but it was always an adventure with my dad. He had a wariness of roots. Never wanted to stay in one place for long."

"How about you? Do you want to move around like that?"

"I liked it with him. Everything new excited him incredibly. New places, new projects, even new toxics. He was insatiably curious about everything. I miss the passion of working with him." Shay fell silent for a moment. "I miss him. A lot."

Anthea couldn't think of anything to say, so she was relieved to see Adrian waving from the curb. He looked strange in jeans and a T-shirt under a close-fitting leather jacket. His jeans had razor-sharp creases — *ah, that's my Adrian*. She pulled over and Shay got out, turned around and moved into the back seat.

Anthea saw Adrian's arched eyebrows as he glanced at Shay. She ignored his knowing wink. She introduced them and then let Adrian guide her.

"Left here. This, my dear, is Castro Street. And there's my favorite coffee store, Cliff's has the best hardware and there's A Different Light, and look out this side. That bar, don't ever go in there. The men are so sleazy."

Shay perched right in the gap behind the bucket seats. "How would you know?"

132

Adrian glanced back at Shay, then looked at Anthea. "I thought you said she was shy."

"I — uh —"

Shay suddenly yelled, "Stop! Pull over!" Anthea swerved to the curb. "Roll down the window," she told Adrian, then leaned forward, squeezing herself past Adrian in a spine-wrenching contortion. Adrian was shoved into Anthea's lap.

"If she's picking up a girl, I'll kill her," Adrian said.

"Women, not girls," Anthea said. She peered past Adrian to see what Shay was doing.

She was shouting and waving her arms. "Hey, it's me. I didn't know you lived around these parts."

Adrian said, "If she doesn't introduce me, I'll kill her."

Anthea finally managed to see that Shay was talking to a man — a very good-looking black man with shoulders the width of Canada.

"Let's make this more civilized," Adrian said. "Scoot back." Shay moved and Adrian opened the door to let Shay out. He then lingered.

"It's old home week," Shay said. "Harold, this is Anthea from my car pool, and this is Adrian, who works with Anthea. And we are collectively, I'm sure, the entire complement of gay people foolish enough to work at NOC-U."

Anthea leaned over, nodded, said hello. Adrian shook hands — took his time over it, Anthea noticed — and said pleased to meet you. Shay explained their reason for being there while Harold offered pieces of the muffins he'd just gotten at the bakery. Adrian, standing with one foot up on the running board, commented on how small a world it was and how amazing it was that he and Harold hadn't run into each other before because Adrian would have certainly remembered if they had.

Anthea managed not to gag. Then she had to congratulate Adrian for his gung ho attitude. She realized abruptly that she had the same intentions toward Shay that Adrian had toward Harold. He was just being more obvious about it. Her nerves jangled. She wanted a cigarette. A lot. *You are a nonsmoker.* Keep saying that, she told herself. She had deliberately not been counting them or the days that had gone by since she had had one. She wanted one now and that meant she hadn't yet quit. She wondered if she would ever stop wanting one.

"Where are you taking us to dinner, Anthea sweetheart?" Adrian leaned down to smile blandly at her. She had never thought she would see Adrian in cowboy boots.

"Your choice."

"When?"

"I don't know. Whenever we've got the car and have had our joyride."

"Six?"

Anthea said that was fine and watched as Adrian turned back to Harold — and ostensibly Shay — and invited him to join them for dinner at someplace called the Rusty Onion at six. Shay seemed very pleased, so Anthea supposed she didn't mind. Shay returned to the back seat and then Adrian stumbled into the car.

"These clodhopper feet," he muttered. "He didn't see me, did he?"

"Your reputation for grace is secure," Anthea said scathingly. "I never realized your feet were so big."

"They're huge," he said morosely, then he brightened. "I actually met a new man. Thanks, Shay," he said over his shoulder.

Anthea said testily, "I presume I need to pull back out into traffic?"

"Please," he said, then he directed her to turn right and left until she had lost all sense of direction. He finally told her to pull over in front of a small apartment building off a narrow one-way street.

Adrian returned in about ten minutes, just as Anthea was getting anxious.

"He says to pull the car out of the garage and put yours in its place while we go for a drive. And if you don't want it, he'll understand. He gave me the check and pink slip to hold until you make up your mind."

"I was hoping he would come with us," Anthea said.

Adrian shook his head. "He's . . . having a bad day. He wanted to come out too, but there's no way." Adrian had a tight look around his eyes. Then he smiled and swung a key in front of her. "Let's go get the baby."

Anthea left the Legend's flashers on and then hurried after Adrian and Shay who were lifting a garage door.

"Wow," Shay said. "This is fabulous."

Anthea crept up behind Shay and whispered, "I'm in love with my car."

It was everything Adrian had promised. In the

dim light of the garage, Anthea imagined that it winked at her. The top was pristine white, gleaming against the brilliant red finish of the exterior. In full light, Anthea was sure the shine would be blinding. The license plate read "IBPROUD."

Adrian unlocked the driver's door and bowed like a valet. "Madam, your carriage awaits."

White leather. The seat made welcoming noises as she oozed down into it. Vintage dials, recessed into the trademark flat dashboard of a Volkswagen, gleamed chrome at her. The dashboard and carpet were black.

"I'm in love with my car," Anthea said again. "Let's go for a ride."

"Top down, milady?"

"Definitely." She was attentive while Adrian showed her how the top folded behind the back seat.

"I have instructions if you decide you want it."

"Of course I want it."

"We'll see once you get it out on the road. Oh, in the trunk —" He went to the front of the car — "is the removable tape deck and the best cruising music ever, I'm told." He rummaged and emerged grinning. "The Stones. Let's boogie."

Adrian volunteered to ride shotgun and Anthea glanced at Shay with a giggle of excitement. She turned the key gently in the ignition and the VW sprang to life. With the greatest of care, she backed out of the garage.

Shay leapt out with Anthea's keys and quickly moved the Legend into the garage. "All stowed away, Captain," she said as she swung back into the passenger seat.

"Impulse speed, then." She eased the clutch out

and the VW purred down the alley. Following Adrian's directions, they cruised slowly back to Castro Street with "Jumpin' Jack Flash" blaring from the speakers. Anthea concentrated on driving while Shay and Adrian waved as if they were in the Rose Parade. Still following Adrian's directions they proceeded down Market to Van Ness, then managed a stately drive past Opera Plaza.

"Let's test the gears," Adrian said. "When I tell you to turn right, we're going to go up some steep hills. Think you can do it?"

"I'll try." She drove cautiously and when the time came, shifted down into first and slowly climbed the steep blocks, managing each time to get the front tires on the flat of the cross street. Congratulating herself when they reached the top, she zipped across the intersection.

With a yelp, she braked. The road appeared to drop away into nothing.

"Trust me," Adrian said. "Go forward just a little."

She wanted to close her eyes. The car tipped forward and she realized where she was. "I've never done this before!" She turned the wheel to accommodate the brick-lined curves of Lombard Street.

Shay was bracing herself away from the dash. "I've always wanted to drive down this street because it isn't straight."

Before the afternoon was over, they had driven across the Golden Gate and back, cut a blazing swath through clogged traffic at Fisherman's Wharf and wended their way back to the Castro where Shay and Adrian, in Anthea's opinion, behaved like children seat-dancing to "Satisfaction." It was just before six when Anthea parked not too far from the restaurant Adrian had picked out.

Shay's hair was standing on end. Anthea liked the effect. Her own neat braid was unchanged, though the rear view mirror showed that the hair at her temples was curlier than usual and her cheeks were red from the wind. Anthea decided she hadn't had this much fun in years, if ever.

The Rusty Onion was not the kind of restaurant Anthea would have chosen, but she didn't mind it. Beer signs adorned the walls and both music and voices assaulted her ears as they entered. True to her albeit limited experience, the bar was lined with men, but they paid her no attention. Harold, however, was ogled as they all trooped by. He didn't seem to mind.

The dining area was a little quieter and Shay sighed as they sat down. "Somebody serving me dinner for once — I like it."

"You deserve it," Anthea said. "This dinner is on me so everybody order whatever you'd like."

"That's not necessary," Harold said. "After all —"

"No arguing at the dinner table," Anthea said primly, then she smiled at Harold to show she was joking. He grinned back and gave her a nod of acquiescence.

"Mmm," Shay said. "By the way, I decided I

could afford to cut back on the pizza parlor. I'll only be working Tuesdays, Wednesdays, Thursdays and Saturdays starting next week. It was that or go completely crazy. I'm almost debt free."

"Congratulations," Anthea said. "You'll be a new woman." She wondered what Shay was like when she wasn't tired all the time. More of everything, she thought. Funnier, cuter and . . . everything.

Their waiter materialized suddenly, leaning close to Adrian and Harold. "Cock-tails?" He batted his eyelashes. "You're supposed to laugh. It's my favorite line."

Adrian said, "Shall we split a carafe of wine?"

Shay glanced at her, and Anthea quickly said, "If you'd like, please do, but none for me, thanks."

"You're the designated driver then, honey," the waiter said. Shay deferred to Adrian and Harold and they decided, after a great deal of discussion, on a white wine with a French name that made the waiter give an excited squeak. "Ex-cellent choice, my dears, I'll be back in two shakes of a queen's tail."

"I work with someone for five years," Adrian said, "and I never realized you don't drink, though I can guess why. What else don't I know about you, Andy?"

"Lots of things." Anthea decided to explain. "My parents were alcoholics. I don't know if I don't drink because they drank and I hated what it did to them or if I'm afraid I'll follow in their footsteps."

There was a short silence, then Shay said, "My father smoked himself to death, so I know I'll never touch them. It's probably the same thing."

"Let's not talk about death and diseases," Adrian said. "Let's talk about something amusing."

"Like NOC-U?" Harold leaned forward on the table, crossing his powerful arms. "It's a deeply weird place."

"We can't talk about work, either," Adrian said. "We can always get together for lunch at the Cafe Ptomaine any day of the week and talk about work."

"Work and dying," Anthea said with a smile. "What else is there? Should we talk about taxes?"

"You people," Adrian said in disgust. "What about art? Film? Opera? Theater? You know, the things that make life worth living?"

"So that's why my life is the pits," Shay said. The restaurant was on the dark side and Anthea thought Shay looked absolutely marvelous. Her eyes glinted like onyx. "All I do is work, think about dying and worry about what they're doing with my taxes. Would seeing *Aida* change all that?"

"With the right cast," Adrian said.

"I need supertitles at the opera," Harold said.

"Supertitles?" Adrian sounded shocked. "You have not been going to the opera with the right people, obviously."

Shay looked at Anthea. "Do you have any idea what they're talking about?"

Anthea nodded. "I used to date someone who loved opera."

Their wine was served and they ordered appetizers and dinner. Shay and Harold both ordered "real" meals, as Harold called them, while Anthea and Adrian chose lighter dishes.

"A salad is just what I need," Anthea said. "Us sedentary office types need to watch our waistlines."

Harold looked Adrian up and down. "I hadn't

140

noticed," he said. Anthea noticed Shay looking at her and nodding, and she fought down a blush. First, Mrs. Giordano had called it a date and now Harold and Adrian were carrying on like adolescents. What would Shay think?

"Flatterer," Adrian said. "Flattery will get you anywhere, you know."

"Down, boys," Anthea said.

"Too late," Harold said. Adrian laughed.

"This place is bringing out their hormones," Shay said. "And here I'd been thinking we probably represented the upper two percent of NOC-U's available I.Q. Are the people in your department as stupid as the people we work with?"

"I thought we weren't going to talk about work," Harold said.

"I don't know," Anthea said. "Nobody stays long enough to tell."

"Let's ignore them," Adrian said. He turned to face Harold. "Seen any good movies lately?"

Shay said to Anthea, "It's just a feeling I have. The only people on our project who know their jobs are the word processors who are so understaffed I waited almost four days for my report to be formatted and printed out . . . it's eighty pages, but still, four days is a long time. My supervisor's had it now for another week. Lord knows what he's doing with it. He thought the well results were a mistake. He's very good at writing and following procedures, and filling out paperwork. But he doesn't know diddly about toxic waste or environmental engineering. All the engineers seem to be very weak scientists."

"Sounds typically NOC-U," Anthea said. She sipped the iced tea she had ordered. "Competence is expensive."

Shay gave a short, unamused laugh. "Not necessarily ... I saw the payroll sheet once. These dummies are not cheap to the company. It's so bad I keep thinking it's deliberate."

"Deliberate? Why would they do it deliberately?"

"To make it look like they're spending money on groundwater control while they do absolutely nothing."

"But that would be wrong."

Shay looked at Anthea, and blinked several times. After a moment, she said, "I've worked on a lot of cleanup sites. You'd be surprised at how much company management will lie, cheat and steal to avoid spending money on cleanups. They'll go to almost any lengths."

"But if they knew about it, surely they'd do something."

"If the managers of industrial firms cared about people and the earth more than profits, maybe. But that's just not the case."

Anthea stared at her glass for a few minutes. "Maybe it's just incompetence. It does seem to rise to the top at NOC-U. The people I've seen promoted surprise me."

"They promote people with the same thinking. It's self-perpetuating." Shay leaned back in her chair and stretched her legs.

Anthea concentrated on what Shay was saying to keep herself from staring. Trim and muscular, these legs were not the kind that usually attracted her. Lois had jogged regularly, but her legs weren't as slender. She didn't know how Shay kept them that way when she didn't have a spare moment to run.

"I've seen two kinds of management styles in toxic-producing corporations. The incompetents who truly thought that if they ignored the problem it would go away. And then there are the people I'd say are truly evil who add up the numbers and decide other people's lives are less important than the money. So they do nothing or they dump in someone's backyard. And when the EPA catches them they use lawsuits and appeals to keep on doing nothing. And then they try bankruptcy and the people who let everything go that long take their golden parachutes and someone else gets to deal with it."

"— it's her favorite speech," Harold was saying. "Next comes the part about the rainforest and global warming."

Shay glared at Harold. "Anthea is a complete innocent about toxic waste. And NOC-U produces it. It's an oil refinery, for God's sake."

Adrian arched his eyebrows at Shay. "I knew the moment I saw you that you were a despoiler of innocents. I should take Anthea away from your influence."

"I'm not an innocent," Anthea said. "But I guess I never really thought about it." She suddenly felt stupid and gauche. "I keep forgetting what NOC-U makes. All I ever see are numbers and volumes. I'm an accountant, not an engineer."

"You sound like Dr. McCoy," Harold said.

"You could be an accountant for lots of other companies," Shay said. "Nonprofits would be thrilled to have you, even in this lousy job market."

143

The very idea of looking for another job frightened Anthea. Wasn't she better off with a situation she knew? "Next you'll be calling NOC-U the patriarchy," she said with a smile.

"It is," Shay and Adrian said simultaneously. They grinned at each other.

"Andy," Adrian said, "haven't you ever noticed that there's only one woman on the board of directors? She happens to be the only person of color, too." Anthea flushed. She felt picked on. It must have shown in her face because Adrian added, "I'd die if you didn't work there. And any semblance of the corporation's knowing anything about what anything costs would cease to be."

"Not that there's any correlation between cost and price of goods," Anthea said. "Our unit's only function is to make sure the profit margin exists. I've always known that. It just never bothered me before."

"Innocence lost," Adrian said. He looked at Harold. "I remember when it happened to me."

"You must tell me about it."

"They're at it again," Shay said in a whisper to Anthea. "I haven't seen this much flirting since lunchtime in junior high."

Anthea offered to give Harold a lift home, which he accepted, and the Bug hummed its way up a steep alley off Castro Street. In one fluid motion, Harold vaulted from the back seat to the curb. Adrian applauded.

Shay said, "I'll see you tomorrow," but Harold

didn't seem to hear her. Instead, he was writing his work extension number down for Adrian.

Adrian took the piece of paper and, while looking up at Harold, said, "Tell me. Is it true what they say about black men?"

Harold leaned on the car and looked down at Adrian's feet. "Is it true what they say about the size of a man's feet?"

"Oh my," Adrian said. "It's true."

Anthea shrieked and covered her face with her hands.

Shay said, "Do you think that if you tried you could be any less subtle?"

Harold said to Adrian, "Women are such prudes."

Anthea let out the clutch and the little car shot away, leaving Harold waving. Adrian and Shay waved back until they turned the corner.

"Sorry I embarrassed you," Adrian said, leaning forward. Anthea didn't think he sounded in the least bit sorry. "Believe me, that was tame compared to what I've heard has gone on in this car. These little stains back here, for instance —"

"I don't want to know," Anthea said. What on earth was Shay thinking, she wondered.

Maybe the car's past would rub off on Anthea, Shay thought. Maybe when they were finally alone in the car, she'd ravish her and make passionate, thorough love to her. The Legend was a nice car, but it hardly inspired the libido.

There. She had finally admitted exactly what she wanted Anthea to do. And she wanted to return the passion. She wanted Anthea to be aggressive and demanding. And why, she asked herself, did she want the one thing Anthea was least likely to do? She was so . . . feminine.

They reclaimed Anthea's Acura from the garage and Adrian said he was going to spend some time with his friend and would find his own way home. He gave Anthea the pink slip and then waved them away.

Shay offered to lead the way to the Bay Bridge, since Anthea had no idea where she was, then Anthea would take over and Shay would follow her. With Adrian's help they put the top up and Shay kept a lookout for the VW's round headlights behind her as they drove away.

She didn't put great store in creature comforts. She'd lived in too many less developed areas to think an expensive car was the be-all and end-all of existence. Still, there was something to say for a car that was in good working condition and that sported a 20 CD mixer and wall-to-wall sound. A stereo like this would drown out the Horizon's bad cylinder. She enjoyed the experience of driving a car that probably cost as much as what she'd make this year, knowing she wasn't likely to repeat it. And now that she thought about it, this car would probably provide room for agile people to try new things. She told herself not to think about it, but it was like someone telling you not to think of a white bear. The more she told herself to think about anything but making love to Anthea the more she thought about Anthea's hands and legs and hips and thighs.

When she'd first met Anthea, Shay had thought her cold. Pleasant, but emotionless. The first time she had genuinely laughed, Shay had been startled. After that she had gone out of her way to make Anthea laugh. She forced herself to face facts. She might be able to get Anthea to laugh, but Anthea would never bubble or chatter. And Shay had always been attracted to bubbly, voluble women. In fact, Anthea was a hundred and eighty degrees different from the kind of woman Shay usually lusted after.

The VW passed her on the Bay Bridge and Shay changed lanes to follow it. They didn't take I-80, much to Shay's surprise, since that was the way they always went home from work. Instead, they went through the MacArthur Maze, and dropped down onto 24, which would eventually take them through the Caldecott Tunnel to Orinda and Walnut Creek. She assumed they'd get off the freeway long before that. Anthea could hardly live in the height of the Claremont district.

At the last exit before the tunnel, she followed Anthea off the freeway, then eventually found herself behind the Claremont Hotel. They wound up some fairly steep streets, but the Legend had no trouble with them. Shay wondered if her Horizon could make it. They were going right up to the top. Where rich people lived.

Anthea turned left into a driveway and Shay pulled in behind her. "Wow," she said, as she handed over Anthea's keys. "You must have an incredible view."

"Come take a look," Anthea said, as Shay had hoped she would. She'd try not to drool on anything. "Would you like some coffee or tea," Anthea asked as she unlocked the front door.

"Tea would be nice," Shay said. "Oh my." She

stood still, staring around the entryway. As Anthea turned the lights on, Shay fell in love with the light oak hardwood parquet that gave way to a pale rose carpet in the living room. The shades of color in the wallpaper were subtle, like Anthea's moods. Shay couldn't believe she'd once thought Anthea moody. "This is like something out of *Architectural Digest*." The furniture was a simple, clean style — subtle geometries at work, no floral prints. Shay was willing to bet it hadn't come from Sears.

"It is nice, isn't it? The view is this way." Anthea unlocked the sliding glass door that led to a deck. "It didn't used to be so good, but the fire took all the trees. Now you can see much better, but I'd rather have the trees back."

Shay stood in awe. Through the hazy dark she could see the Golden Gate, the Bay Bridge and all of the Oakland estuary. She was actually looking down on the Claremont Hotel. Her knees suddenly felt weak, and she dropped into a chair at the patio table. Anthea wasn't comfortably well off. She was rich.

Anthea returned with china teacups — on saucers, no less. Shay sipped timidly from her cup and discovered it was not as delicate as it looked, so she relaxed. Anthea had money, but it wasn't an insurmountable obstacle. "It's so quiet," she said. "Just the crickets and an occasional car."

"For a while after the fire there weren't even the crickets. I stood here at night and it was kind of creepy. But they're back. When it isn't so hazy, I can see Sausalito. It's kind of limited tonight."

"I'll take it," Shay said. She wondered what Anthea would do if Shay suggested spreading a blanket out on the deck and...she clenched her thighs. Oh, dear. Think about a white bear, she told herself.

"We need music," Anthea said. "I'll find something."

By the time Anthea returned, Shay could hear the swelling tones of Stomu Yamashta. She relaxed even further. She used to meditate to music like this.

"I don't think I'd ever leave home," Shay said. She tipped her head back and looked at the stars. She imagined Anthea standing over her, leaning down, kissing her. *White bear. White bear.* She closed her eyes against the vision and clenched the arms of her chair.

What seemed only moments later there was a soft touch on her shoulder. Shay sat bolt upright, shocked that she had actually fallen asleep. Anthea retreated.

"I'm sorry, I thought you'd get a horrible crick in your neck if I let you sleep much longer."

Shay twisted her neck around. It had a familiar ache, the kind of ache it had after she'd spent a considerable amount of time between...don't start that again, she chided herself. *White bear.* Don't start. *White bear.* Her body felt as if she'd been in a hot tub. What on earth had she been dreaming about? The sensation between her legs...she'd obviously been dreaming about sex. Probably about Anthea. *Oh, great.*

"Thanks," she managed to say. "What time is it?"

"Ten-thirty."

"Oh." It was time for all good guests to go home. Argh. She stood up. "I can't believe I was so rude."

"Mrs. Giordano will think I've kept you out too late on a school night," Anthea said. She didn't sound offended.

Shay sat quietly in the passenger seat while Anthea drove the Legend down out of the hills.

"See you tomorrow," Anthea said. "Thank you for helping me get the VW."

"It was fun. And thank you for dinner. That was fun, too." This was the point where Anthea was supposed to suggest they do it again. Shay waited a moment, then felt very awkward, so she started to open her door.

"Shay," Anthea said. Shay turned back. Anthea lightly touched Shay's lips with her own. Shay shivered and let out a tiny moan. Then she realized Anthea would figure out Shay was burning with desire and for some reason it seemed very important to hide that fact. She drew back sharply and bashed her head on the door window.

"I'm sorry," Anthea said. "I didn't mean —"

"No, my fault. I was just surprised."

"I just wanted to thank you —"

"You didn't have to stop —"

"Are you okay?"

"I'm fine." Shay rubbed the back of her head. "I . . . um."

"Well," Anthea said, her face only partially illuminated by the dashboard light, "I'll see you tomorrow morning."

"Yeah. It'll be all too soon." Shay realized how that sounded. "I mean the morning, not seeing you." She remembered she had to proofread her report. It felt like she had been away from work for weeks.

Anthea laughed. Shay had really made a fool of

herself, but at least Anthea had laughed. "I knew what you meant. See you in the morning."

Shay staggered into her apartment and threw herself down on the bed. She rolled over and stared at the ceiling. What an utter fool she had made of herself. She had behaved like a child. Falling asleep . . . how could she have done such a thing? She felt the front of her jeans. At least her fly was buttoned. She threw one arm over her eyes as she upbraided herself. The other hand lazily rubbed the buttons, then she realized she was throbbing underneath the fabric.

Slowly, she unbuttoned her jeans and slid her hand downward and inward, as tantalizing yet direct as she had hoped Anthea would be. She closed her eyes and imagined Anthea's fingers. In the dark, her pulse racing, her fingers slipped through the wetness she wasn't surprised to find. Her heart rate soared with her passion.

7

Slippery When Wet

Shay seemed reticent to Anthea, but maybe she just hadn't slept well. Anthea had slept miserably. Lois had been right — she was so boring she had put Shay to sleep. And then Shay had practically killed herself trying to avoid a kiss. Obviously she wasn't Shay's type and she'd only embarrassed them both. Meanwhile, last night she had been a mass of libidinous jelly.

She'd fallen in lust enough times to tell herself

that what she felt was normal. It was just like when she had fallen for Lois...sure it was. *And look where that got you.* Anthea let the stab of self-disgust and hurt distract her from the butterflies in her stomach that meant nothing but trouble. Butterflies...no, it was probably just a remnant of last night's supper. *A bit of undigested potato, perhaps.*

She glanced over at Shay and it seemed that Shay wouldn't meet her eyes. Great. *Your libido gets out of hand and you'll be driving to work alone very soon.* It was just as well that Shay wouldn't look at her. Shay's eyes sparkled like a distant galaxy... Anthea reined her thoughts up sharply. No, the fluttering in her stomach was definitely not butterflies, she told herself again.

When they arrived at the parking lot, Shay hurried toward the shuttle stop without a backward glance. Anthea started to slam her car door then realized Shay had left her lunch bag. She swooped it off the floor board and called after Shay.

Shay looked back, then down at what Anthea was carrying as if she couldn't believe that Anthea had her lunch. Anthea saw Shay's shuttle come around the corner, so she ran full tilt toward Shay, hoping Shay would still make it.

Oxygen deprivation made her giddy. "Do you like barbecued steak?" Anthea's words came out in a gasp as she handed over the brown paper bag.

"Yes. Why?" Shay looked back toward the approaching shuttle.

"I love to barbecue but it's such a fuss to do it for just one. Would you like to celebrate your first Friday night off? The start of our three-day weekend? Independence Day and all that? You can see some fireworks from the deck." It didn't come out precisely the way she had practiced it in front of the mirror.

"I'd love to," Shay said. She looked a little startled.

She said yes, Anthea thought. Oh, my God. "What else do you like to eat?"

Shay's mouth hung open for a split second before she answered in a strange voice, "Just about anything. I have to run now."

Shay dropped limply into her chair, praying that no one had noticed her slipping in a few minutes late. "I barely made my shuttle," she gasped to Harold, who was already bent over his keyboard.

"Scott was just here. He left that mess on your desk."

"Damn."

"I told him you were in the bathroom."

"Thank you, sweet prince."

"Think nothing of it. Thanks to you, I'm in love." Harold leaned back in his chair and smiled at her.

Shay couldn't help herself. "So am I," she said, with chagrin.

"He's mine," Harold said in a conspiratorial whisper.

"Don't be disgusting. I wasn't talking about him."

"I see. Well, I did wonder."

"You don't think she could tell, do you?" That Anthea knew how strongly Shay felt was Shay's worst fear.

"You were not being very clear," Harold said. "You just hung on her every word."

"Oh."

"You could try being a little more direct, you know."

"I don't think so. I don't think I'm her type."

"Type? Like S/M? Leather?"

"Not everything is about what you do in bed," Shay said haughtily while parts below her waist called her a liar.

"Why not?" Harold shook his head. "If it doesn't work there, it's not going to work anywhere else."

"If it won't work anywhere else, what's the point of it working in bed?"

Harold stared at her. "You women are so strange." He lowered his voice. "What on earth is wrong with good sex?"

"Nothing, except if the sex is good then it seems like getting married is a logical next step and then you hate each other and break up."

Harold whispered, with a half smile, "Do you know what the majority of the *Sentinel's* women's ads are for? Therapy. Now I know why."

"Chauvinist," she hissed.

Harold smiled angelically. "Why do you think she thinks you're not her type?"

"She's rich. She's white. She's in the closet. She believes in personal emancipation, obviously, but hasn't thought about the rest of the world."

"So teach her."

"I don't think a relationship should be based on someone having to change for it to work. And she's . . . not someone to play with. I think she's been hurt a lot."

"Well, the lady struck me as a survivor. Maybe she has got money and no idea how easy her skin has made life. But you like her so what else matters in the end?"

"Nothing, I guess. We're having dinner on Friday."

"She invited you?" Shay nodded. "Well then, there you are." Harold broke off to answer his phone.

Shay gave herself another moment to savor the fact that she was actually having dinner with Anthea. An official date at Anthea's dream of a house. Barbecuing on that wonderful deck. Then she opened her eyes and looked at what Scott had left. With a sigh, she picked up the thick stack of papers.

Harold hung up the phone and leaned across the cubicle to whisper in Shay's ear, "I hope she fucks your brains out."

Shay gasped and dropped the stack of papers. "Crude, crude and cruder!" Harold just laughed and went back to work.

The papers were a mess, and it had nothing to do with dropping them on the floor. They had been her first draft of the report about the last series of well tests, including the lab data that showed well B-B-146 was approaching the hazardous range for xylene. Her report pointed this out and proposed a schedule of more frequent testing to prepare for remediation, if necessary.

Scott had butchered it. The pages were covered with edits. It would take her all day to transcribe them for the word processors. She sighed, wanting to throw it in the wastebasket. But she was more sure than ever that the lab data was right, so she wasn't going to let it go and assume that the data had been a mistake just because the report would be easier to write.

She worked through lunch again, munching her peanut butter and jelly sandwich in near despair. The edits were blatantly attempting to confuse the issues, converting the succinct style she had learned from her father to an obtuse bureaucratic mess that employed double negatives and lots of unclear antecedents. Whole paragraphs were constructed of a single sentence with clause after clause of obfuscation. And then, to top it off, he'd eliminated the entire section she'd written on remediating the xylene area and removed all mention of the latest well sample. It still showed up in the summary table in Appendix F, but that was it. The longer she worked on it, the angrier she became.

She was not going to let the matter drop. She was not going to give it up. And if they fired her she'd take her copy and the results to the Regional Water Quality Board herself. And she'd go to the media and borrow money from Anthea to live. And then she'd sue.

She took a break, and when she caught a glimpse of herself in the bathroom mirror she smiled at the mulish expression on her face and the way her jaw was jutting forward. Then she realized she looked exactly like her father did when he was preparing for a run-in with management. No, she was not going to let it go.

She took the report over to word processing just before they closed up shop at four o'clock. She apologized to the supervisor for the mess and tried to hint that it was important. The supervisor, a harried black woman who always looked tired, sighed when she saw the amount of work and said they'd do their best. As usual, they would call when it was ready.

The report wasn't ready until Wednesday afternoon. Shay couldn't really blame them for taking so long — it had been a lot of work. The finished documents were put in racks and Shay searched for hers. *Report: First Quarter Sampling.* That was it. Shay picked it up and headed back to her desk.

Halfway there, she realized it wasn't her report. It was based on the data she was using and it had whole paragraphs from her original draft, but the pages were coded with a different document identification number and the job sheet, now that she looked closely, had been filled out by Scott.

She didn't think twice. She went back to the word processing trailer and slipped into the copier room. She duplicated Scott's entire document, then put it back in the word processing rack, mumbling something about having taken the wrong one. She found her version, then duplicated her marked-up draft and the new copy. Then she went back to her desk. Harold wasn't in their cube so Shay sat very still and tried to decide what to do.

Well, Scott had said Shay was to write the report her way. She supposed that didn't preclude Scott from writing his own report, and true, she had not spoken with him about her draft. But the changes he'd made had been deliberately reducing emphasis on the increasing xylene level. She didn't have a choice — she would have to read Scott's version through and figure out how they differed in substance. Then she would decide what to do.

She certainly couldn't do the analysis here. She would have to take it home and work on it after she left the pizza parlor tonight. She strained the worn brown paper of her lunch bag to the limit by curling the copies she had made into it.

Anthea was a little worried that Shay hadn't mentioned their dinner plans all week, but then Shay had looked distracted and exhausted. She could call Shay. There was no reason not to. She thought about it for a few more minutes and then slowly picked up the handset. She dialed Shay's extension, which she had memorized, but never used before, and then Shay answered. Her voice failed her.

"Anyone there?" Shay sounded distracted.

"Hi, it's me. Anthea."

"Oh hi."

"Uh, I just wanted to remind you about tomorrow night."

"I haven't forgotten. Can I bring anything?"

Anthea was flooded with relief. Shay had seemed so distant, and this morning she'd looked as if she hadn't slept at all. "No, no. I have everything. Unless you'd like to drink something."

"Iced tea will suit me just fine, especially if this gorgeous weather holds."

"I'll make up a pitcher, then." She thought she heard Harold's voice . . . something about Shay remembering to bring her brains. Shay said something in a sharp tone and the line went dead.

Her intercom rang while she still held the handset. "Anthea Rossignole," she said, hoping she didn't sound as distracted as she felt.

Adrian's voice came over the line. "I hope you get lucky."

Anthea hung up on him.

Shay fumbled with the buttons on her best blouse, a gift from her father several years ago. She wanted to look nice and the emerald jacquard silk helped. Her hair needed to be cut — it was getting too long for any amount of gel to make it stand up. Her ancient heritage included hair that wouldn't curl no matter what she did to it. It looked like she was wearing a flat tire around her head. She peered closer. Wrinkles. Oh, definitely. Right in the corners of her eyes. Terrific. Take a job in the private sector, she thought, and you age overnight.

Two hours of sleep two nights running hadn't helped her appearance. Harold had noticed her lack of energy and offered advice on ways to boost her energy and stamina — along with more lewd comments. Men, she thought. It's a wonder any woman found them tolerable as more than friends.

She tried another dose of freezing spray and coughed as she sucked some into her lungs. Oh well, it couldn't be any worse than what they breathed on the refinery. Sure, it passed the air quality standards, but one of Shay's teachers had given her a good rule of thumb: if your nose doesn't like the smell of it, you shouldn't be breathing it in. Every day there was some new aroma that her nose didn't like.

Well, she wouldn't be breathing it in for long. Not when she confronted Scott about the report. He'd fire her, she was sure of it. But tonight — tonight she got to relax. Her first Friday night date in years and the start of a three-day weekend.

Her body was prickling with anticipation. Of what, she couldn't say. She didn't know what to expect. Anthea was unlike any woman she'd known before. Misha, for example. Misha had been in a taiko troupe, with the chiseled body of a goddess. She could still remember the way the drums made her heart race, especially watching Misha play the large ones, drums that took the whole body to strike. It distracted her for a moment, and then she compared Misha to Anthea. Anthea was not the athletic type. Anthea was really closeted. But that didn't change the fact that Shay wanted to be with her.

She took one last sighing look at herself in the mirror. She was too thin. Her collar bone was practically sticking out. She hadn't been eating enough protein or getting enough sleep. But she'd put the last payments to the hospital and funeral home in the mail this morning. It seemed like a sign that the very same day she had her first real date with Anthea.

Anthea sat down across the patio table from Shay and raised her glass. "To your more restful future," she said. She tinked her glass against Shay's, and then sipped her cider. She wanted to look cool and calm. Then she dribbled cider down the front of her shirt and onto her new jeans.

She'd been fine until Shay had sat down and a sudden breeze had caught Shay's thin blouse. The fabric billowed, outlining the small breasts and nipples that tightened in the cooling air. The form-fitting 501s left no doubt about how far it was from knee to ... important areas, or how much supple softness Shay's thighs might offer.

"I can't get over how beautiful the view is," Shay said. She got up and went to the railing.

Anthea swallowed a huge lump in her throat. Her mouth was dry, then she was practically drooling. Shay bent slightly, the jeans pulled tight, emphasizing the trim, lean body of a runner. Oh, God, Anthea thought. *She probably thinks I'm fat.* She felt every drop of blood in her body drain to one place which pulsed so hard she thought she would die. *What a way to go.*

"The fireworks will be down thataways at the Coliseum," Anthea said, pointing. "And some at the Port of Oakland. We might see some at the Embarcadero."

Shay turned toward her and her silk-covered arm brushed against the back of Anthea's hand. Anthea felt a jolt and her goblet of sparkling cider went flying over the deck railing. The muffled sound of glass breaking floated up to them.

"Oh, no," Shay gasped. "That was all my fault."

"No, really, it was me. It must mean good luck ... like when people throw their glasses into the fireplace." Anthea was lightheaded from Shay's proximity. *It's a wonder I haven't driven into an embankment some morning.*

Shay said, "I feel just awful. I should replace it."

"No, really, it was all my fault. Let's not dwell on it. It's not as if it were Waterford. Believe me, it's a great deal more modest than that." Anthea was anxious to put Shay at ease again. Suddenly she reached over and grabbed Shay's glass from her hand, then tossed it after the one she'd lost.

"Double good luck," she said.

Shay gaped at her. "I'm staying away from the railing," she said, warily sidling away from Anthea.

As if she were drunk, Anthea felt the world tipping this way and that. She wasn't sure what she would do next. She cast about for something to say, then saw flames leaping up from the grill.

She fished one of the steaks off the rocks. "This has never happened to me before. I'm glad I bought an extra." She stood there for a moment, feeling forlorn, with the crispy steak dangling from the barbecue fork.

"I'm sure I'll have plenty to eat," Shay said, her voice tolerant and kind.

Anthea sighed. Those were not precisely the emotions she wanted to engender in Shay. Well, maybe the neighborhood cats would eat it. She tossed it over the railing after the glasses with a shout of "Mazeltov!" She was gratified that Shay laughed.

Anthea felt as if she spent all evening saying, "Excuse me" and "Sorry" and "I'm usually not this clumsy." They were sitting on the deck, studying the lights. Anthea had two less plates. Her clumsiness had been infectious — it was Shay who'd let the

163

plate of corn on the cob tip just as Anthea leaned over to get the barbecue sauce. The cobs had rolled across the deck and into the garden, leaving them both speechless with laughter.

Nonetheless, it had not been a successful evening. She sensed that Shay was agitated, nervous, like a guest who isn't comfortable. Her own emotions were all over the map. She couldn't exactly say, "Shay, would you mind unbuttoning that shirt two more buttons?" or "I'll die if you don't let me kiss you right now." She'd sound just like some guy.

But she wanted Shay so much that she was frightened. She had only been with four women in her life, not counting the Porsche, and they had been very similar in their approach to lovemaking. Lois had said she was boring. Anthea had no idea what Shay liked. What if she wanted the first time to be soft and slow and right now Anthea didn't think she could do slow and soft? And why was she thinking about sex when she wasn't even sure Shay liked her? And why was she thinking about Lois?

"I'm doing it again," Shay said. "I'm about to fall asleep. What a terrible guest I am."

"I guess my powers of conversation have lagged a little."

"No, it's not you," Shay said. "I didn't get much sleep the last two nights. I. . . ." She hesitated.

Anthea prompted her. "Why?"

"There's this report I had to analyze. And . . . well, I could be unemployed very soon." Anthea saw Shay's jaw harden — she'd never seen her look so determined.

"Why is that?"

"I think my boss is trying to cover up a

164

hazardous level of xylene in one of the groundwater samples I took. I found a second version of the report I've been working on, only it doesn't mention the unexpected increase in the xylene level."

"How is it happening? The xylene, I mean."

Shay caught her upper lip between her teeth, then sighed. "I don't know. I can't figure out where the xylene is coming from. It shouldn't be in the groundwater at all, but tanks and pipes leak. This sudden jump tells me there's a tank leak but there isn't a tank nearby. That makes it doubly confusing. The tanks are on the other side of the refinery."

Anthea tried to take it in. She sat up. "And your boss is trying to hide it? How can he get away with that?"

"Dumb luck. He's insisting it's a lab error, but I don't think so. So he leaves it out of the report summary, but presents the data tables intact to the Water Board. Then he hopes that the Regional Water Board is so understaffed that the report is all that will get studied. It happens. It's a crime. The reporting mode at NOC-U is to bury the public safety boards with paperwork. They get discouraged and don't read as closely as they should — they're only human. Meanwhile, a carcinogen gets closer to the clean water channel. And it's not just NOC-U. It's all toxic-producing industry in general."

"How did you find out?"

"The idiot left his version in word processing pickup long enough for me to stumble over it. And I think I'm the only person out there who would see what was happening. They've vastly underrated my scientific background. To them, I'm just a well-digger and a sample taker."

Anthea couldn't believe it was true. She just couldn't. "Are you a hundred percent sure the lab was right? Shouldn't you take another sample?"

"I'd love to, but last time I checked they cost two fifty a pop. I don't have that kind of money to throw away on a maybe. Not when I know the lab result is right."

Anthea felt cold. She chose her words carefully. "If what you say is correct, I've just realized I trust you more than I do NOC-U." She flushed with anger. "All that bullshit about safety records and how they care about the endangered hoot owl. More than anyone, I should know that they spent more on the ad production than they did on the owls, and then they only spent it to comply with a court order. Let's be sure. Really sure. I'll pay for the lab test."

"But Anthea, I don't know if I can get another sample. And we have to move fast because of the reporting deadline."

"Let them file a false report." She stood up and went to the railing. The sun was only an orange line beyond the Golden Gate Bridge. Shay joined her. "Have I been blind? Am I really this naive?"

Shay was silent for a moment, then she said, "Naive about motives, maybe. And I think they've gone to great lengths to shelter people in the Executive Building from the rest of the refinery. So you don't wonder. Or care."

"I care . . . or I thought I did. I've been all over that refinery. I've seen production up close. And somehow I keep forgetting what's being produced. They're necessary products. They're things that we want to buy and make our quality of life what it is. It's very easy to say we should all be riding horses but unless we *all* ride horses no one's going to do it."

Shay nodded. "Conservation is good for the masses, but if the elite don't support it nothing changes. I know that as well as anybody. It's hard for a lay person to get mentally involved. Environmental issues are incredibly complex because it can get down into molecular analysis." Shay absently scratched behind one ear. "If NOC-U is forced to remediate the soil in that area, there are at least seven different theories of how to go about it. The average person can't get into that no matter how much they care."

"You're making me feel less selfish. I truly feel as if I've been sleepwalking all my life."

"You had other things to think about," Shay said. "You didn't grow up with a madman who talked biology in his sleep."

Anthea felt a wave of warmth for Shay. She was being so . . . supportive. Shay put her hand on Anthea's bare arm. A flash of heat sparked from Shay's hand, up Anthea's arm and settled in her stomach. If there had been any ice left from Lois's departure, this heat would have melted it.

"I'd bring your father back if I could," Anthea murmured. "But I can't. So I haven't had a cigarette in three weeks. Or is it four?" Shay's hands moved to her shoulders. Anthea touched Shay's arms, feeling for the first time sinewy biceps and hard muscle in a woman's body. None of her lovers had been like Shay. Anthea never would have guessed that Shay's physique would have made her knees weak. Slender, small-breasted, short, dark. Had it been hidden racism that she had never intimately touched nonwhite skin before? Anthea shook away the thought, unsure of how to resolve it.

She continued her exploration. Shay didn't protest. In fact, her hands had dropped to Anthea's waist. Anthea put one finger on Shay's lips and the contrast of their darkness with her pale skin sent a tremor through her body.

"Your skin is beautiful," she said. Her fingers feathered over Shay's cheeks and nose, then her ears and neck.

"So is yours," Shay said. Anthea heard her swallow. "Are you ever going to kiss me properly?" Anthea nodded and Shay's mouth curved in a soft smile. "Well, I'm ready when you are."

Anthea hadn't expected to feel so powerful. Shay was the one without a single ounce of spare flesh on her body — all that muscle and strength. But from somewhere inside her, Anthea felt a surge of eroticism because of the differences in their bodies. She bent Shay in her arms, tipped her head back and kissed her: a kiss that was all Anthea kissing Shay and Shay's tiny moan, her body arching up against Anthea.

Shay opened her mouth. Her hand at the back of Anthea's neck urged Anthea to explore her. Anthea forgot to breathe for a long minute, then ended the kiss with a gasp for air.

"Oh, my," Shay murmured. "That was . . . very nice."

Anthea cleared her throat. "I thought so, too."

Shay put her hands on Anthea's shoulders and pushed herself easily up onto the deck railing. Anthea clutched at her. "Don't fall."

"I won't," Shay said. "I just wanted to be taller

for a minute." She drew Anthea between her knees and looked down into Anthea's face. Her eyes, wells of glistening darkness, focused on Anthea's lips. Anthea heard a sigh, a half-caught breath, then she lost track of time. Sweet tension. She wanted to press her lips harder against Shay's, devour her mouth. She clenched her fingers around the tiny waist, pulling Shay's weight toward her. She felt passion building in her stomach with waves of fluttering excitement.

Shay arched against Anthea's hip and Anthea turned slightly, inviting Shay's hand to leave her shoulder and move lower. She didn't want to end this kiss, but Shay finally raised her head. Breathlessly she slipped her fingers under the thin fabric of Anthea's tank top. Anthea moaned — she could feel a rhythm in her hips, something like an electric bass. Pulsing and low.

Her fingers were a tangle as she struggled with the buttons of Shay's blouse. Shay's hand pushed against the tight confines of Anthea's bra. Anthea pushed Shay's open blouse away, admiring the small breasts that dimpled in the cool air.

Shay's fingers closed on Anthea's nipple as Anthea engulfed one breast in her mouth. Anthea savored the flesh, devouring the soft hardness with a long groan. She heard a tiny cry from Shay and came back to herself.

"I'm sorry," she gasped.

"No . . . you surprised me." Shay pushed the bra and tank top straps off Anthea's shoulders, peeling them downward. She cupped Anthea's breasts in her hands and said, "Please, go back to what you were doing . . . please."

Anthea felt the bass in her hips surge into a grinding beat. She meant to be gentle but found herself devouring Shay's breasts again in needing desperation. Fingers captured and teased her own aching nipples which felt heavy and engorged. A groan wrenched from her own throat.

They were down on the deck. Anthea didn't think she had fallen there, but somehow she was on her back and Shay's hands were everywhere — at her zipper, on her breasts, holding her head still for another long, breathless kiss. Anthea lifted her hips so Shay could pull her jeans down, then managed to unbutton Shay's jeans. She found her hand slid easily across Shay's smooth stomach. She surprised herself by not stopping, not teasing, her fingers sliding directly between Shay's thighs.

Shay must have been surprised, too. She shuddered and ground her hips toward Anthea's seeking hand. In the darkness, Shay's body was an unfamiliar blur lost in the shadows, but this wetness was familiar. Any anxiety she had about what Shay might want faded. She knew what to do — listen, feel, respond, dance with the new rhythm of Shay's hips arching and straining against her fingertips.

Shay shoved her jeans down, providing more room for Anthea's hand. Anthea struggled upright to pull Shay against her, finding a better angle, the wetness sliding around her fingers. Then she paused, waiting, unsure.

Shay's eyes were closed. She bit her lower lip, then opened her eyes. Her hips moved in tiny flutters.

Anthea moved her fingers toward the source of

the wonderful slipperiness . . . a slight motion that made Shay nod her head. "Yes," she said.

Shay surrendered without protest, something she had never done before. Shay had found that her lovers — infrequent though they were — expected her to take the lead. And she did, giving before she took. She didn't know why. But this surrender to Anthea was so much the sweeter. She managed to kick one leg free of her jeans, then she lifted her hips, saying *deeper* and *yes* without words. Saying *more* and *harder* with her arching back and a flutter of one hand.

Anthea was breathing hard. Shay could hear the short gasps tinted with a moan back in her throat.

Shay slammed both fists against the deck under her, fighting against losing what was left of her emotional distance from Anthea. How could she. . . . Anthea murmured something and Shay seized her shoulders, gripping them as hard as she could, while fierce contractions clenched her muscles tighter, until a brilliant quartz shimmered behind her eyelids.

She slumped to the deck, sobbing for breath. Her head felt like lead. The rest of her body felt unreal. God, she thought. Harold was right.

She realized Anthea was shaking as she withdrew her fingers. Shay pulled the damp hand to her breast with a sigh of pleasure.

Anthea whispered, "Stay the night with me."

"You couldn't make me leave," Shay answered.

Anthea led her to the bedroom Shay had

glimpsed earlier. After flinging back the covers, Anthea fumbled with her clothing — tank top and bra bunched around her waist, jeans barely clinging to her hips — but Shay stopped her with a touch on the shoulder.

"No, leave them like that. You . . . you look so wild. Your hair. . . ." She filled her hands with soft strands, then buried her face in them, rubbing them like silk against her lips. Her lips found skin and she brushed Anthea's hair out of the path of her mouth as she kissed the pliant flesh.

She wrapped her hands around one warm, ivory breast. So soft, she marveled, and so much for her mouth to savor and enjoy. She brushed the tip of her tongue over the rose-tinted nipple. Unexpectedly, Anthea swayed.

She sank to the bed and Shay knelt on the floor in front of her, her tongue returning to the tender swell that grew harder against her tongue. She sighed deeply, feeling languid and hedonistic as she feasted on Anthea's breasts . . . a prelude to another feast on even more sensuous flesh.

Shay pulled Anthea's clothes from her hips. Her head spun as she first saw the dark blonde hair triangled between Anthea's thighs. She rested her forehead for a moment on the pale thatch, inhaling the scent of what she would soon taste.

Recovering from her faintness, she pulled the clothes the rest of the way off. Anthea's legs spread open. Shay promised herself she would give Anthea as much pleasure as she had already received. She would do it slowly, make it last a long time. She thought this even as she lowered her mouth to the triangle of blonde hair. She slipped her tongue into the ready wetness she found, heard Anthea gasp.

She would go slowly, she told herself. Her tongue flicked and Anthea shuddered. She knew Anthea would like that and she would go slow. Slower, she told herself, even as her body sank between Anthea's legs, her arms winding around Anthea's hips. Her lips encircled the nerves knotted and pulsing under her tongue.

Slow was impossible.

She made the second time last longer, but her mouth was so hungry and eager she couldn't restrain her desire for more. Her fingers slipped into Anthea's heat and passion and Anthea's hands pressed Shay's head down. Her hands said stay there, like that, just like that.

8
Fast Lane

Shay felt a wet splash on her forehead and she brushed at it. She wanted to go on sleeping . . . she was melted into the bed. Even as she drifted off, she wondered how her bed had become so soft. And so wide.

There was another droplet, on her cheek this time. She wiped it away and cracked her eyes open. They felt as if they'd been soldered shut.

Anthea stood at the door to her bathroom,

toweling her hair vigorously. Another drop from the fierce whirl of the towel fell onto Shay's face. She sighed. The toweling immediately stopped.

"Did I wake you?" Anthea asked. "I was trying so hard to be quiet."

"It's okay. I don't want to miss you getting dressed." Shay wished Anthea weren't wearing a bathrobe. All in a rush she remembered the abandon and oblivion of the previous night. She curled into a ball and smiled.

"I don't have to get dressed," Anthea said. A subtle flush crept up her cheeks. Shay felt a similar flush in her own body. She wanted to do it all again.

"Not at all," Shay said. "You're ahead of me by a shower, though." She sat up, glancing at the bedside clock. Eight-thirty. She had to be at work in three and a half hours. That left plenty of time for . . . anything. She sniffed. "I need one, too."

"Why don't you help yourself, and I'll make some breakfast."

Shay was glad of the promise of breakfast as she stood wobbly-legged in the shower. Anthea had left her absolutely drained. She felt as weak as a day-old puppy when she finally stepped out of the steam. She found another robe and followed a tantalizing smell to the kitchen.

Anthea was busily mincing green chilies next to the huge double sink. Shay decided that the island alone was bigger than the floor space of her entire kitchen. A copper bowl with what looked like beaten eggs stood next to a shallow copper omelet pan. "Spanish omelets?" From the porcelain crock on the kitchen island, Shay helped herself to a strawberry and dipped it into the whipped cream sitting next to them. Her taste buds went wild — tart, sweet, creamy, decadent.

"I hope you like them," Anthea said. "Would you rather have jack or cheddar?"

"I'd rather have you," Shay said. She gulped. That wasn't what she had meant to say at all. It was a little too early in the morning for high passion.

Anthea dropped the knife and flushed bright red. She picked the knife up again with a little laugh. "You've already had me."

Shay moved behind Anthea, wrapping her arms around Anthea's waist. "I mean to do it again." She felt her stiffen slightly, then relax.

Shay loosened the tie of Anthea's robe. The thin silk was far sexier than the utilitarian chenille Shay wore. She slipped her hands inside. Abundant and luxurious and so soft, Anthea's breasts filled her hands again. "I think you should probably put the knife down," she murmured.

Anthea answered with an incoherent sound, but when she turned to Shay she was empty-handed. Shay only had to bend her head slightly to kiss Anthea's nipples, to pull one into her mouth. She remembered what had made Anthea moan last night . . . a gentle bite, followed by hard pressure from her tongue. The combination made Anthea moan this morning too.

"God, Shay, how can you do this to me?" Anthea threw her shoulders back and Shay took the gesture for encouragement and consent. She slipped to her knees. The dark blonde hair between Anthea's thighs was still damp from her shower, but the wetness was slicker than water.

Shay brushed it with her tongue. Anthea's fingers curled into her hair, gripping so tightly it hurt, but Shay ignored it.

"Slide up on the counter," Shay told her.

There was a clatter. Shay didn't know what had happened to the chilies and she didn't care. Anthea was perched on the edge of the counter and Shay took some of Anthea's weight on her shoulders as she feasted.

It seemed a perfectly appropriate thing to do in the kitchen. Anthea must have thought so too because her body responded almost instantaneously.

They would have to try the dining room at some future date.

Anthea crumpled down from the counter and Shay stood up, capturing Anthea between her body and the counter.

"Okay?" Shay smiled up into Anthea's dazed face.

"Very okay," Anthea answered. "Are you always that . . . hungry?"

"No. And now I'm really starved." She looked longingly at the omelet preparations.

"You don't really expect me to let that go unanswered, do you?" Anthea, some of her color returning, quirked her lips in a sensuous smile. Shay suddenly recalled the softness of those lips on her body.

"No . . . I guess not. I'm hungry for all sorts of things this morning." She felt Anthea's fingers slipping between the folds of the bathrobe. "That, too." She made an appreciative sound as she wrapped her arms around Anthea's neck.

Anthea answered with a sigh. Shay could hear Anthea's steady heartbeat become more rapid as she rested her head on Anthea's chest.

Shay straightened and pushed herself away from Anthea. "I guess turnabout is fair play." She stepped back until she felt the kitchen island against her hips and then pushed herself up onto the island. She spread her legs ... she couldn't pretend to be shy, not after what she'd just done, not after what they'd done on the deck. And there was no pretending she wasn't ready.

Anthea's fingers slipped inside her. Shay felt a warm flush in their wake. She put her hands behind her and rested her weight on them, leaving her hips free to move in response to Anthea's gentle strokes. She met each thrust, bucking against the fingers that sought the fire between her legs. She couldn't stop the long, loud groans that wrenched out of her lungs.

So, she thought, when the tremors had subsided, this is what breakfast with Anthea is like. *I could get used to it.*

She stopped herself there ... so they got along well in bed. As she had told Harold, it took much more to make a relationship. Anthea had seemed inexperienced and shy, but now Shay knew better. She remembered the aggressive dyke she had seen Anthea with ... the one she had called a Porsche. Anthea could be into one night stands even if she didn't look it. Nobody looked like her sex life, Shay thought.

"I think I'll make breakfast now," Anthea said.

Shay sat up, aware that Anthea's shoulder had been very comfortable. She didn't want Anthea to move even a foot away. The burning between her legs persisted; she'd never felt heat like this before. She slid off the kitchen island and wrapped her robe demurely about her body. The heat from her thighs was almost painful. It was painful. When they sat down to eat the omelets, Shay winced. Something was going on. She was wet from Anthea's love-making and from wanting more. But something else . . . she straightened in her chair nonchalantly. She took a bite of omelet. It was delicious. The jack cheese and chilies were mild . . . perfect for breakfast. She ate about half, then couldn't take another bite. The burning sensation was intense. She sat up straight, but it made no difference.

"Are you okay?" Anthea looked across the table in concern.

"Oh, sure."

"Are the chilies too hot?"

"No, uh, they're fine." Shay exhaled rapidly through her nose. "I'm just, I think there's, I. . . ." She didn't know how to say that she thought her body was having some sort of violent reaction to sex. It was terrible. She was allergic to Anthea.

Anthea tipped her head to one side. "Are you sure you're okay? You look odd."

"I don't know what it is," Shay said slowly. How could she explain it? She looked around the kitchen, anywhere but at Anthea. Her embarrassed gaze fell on the remains of the fresh green chilies. *The chilies!* In spite of her embarrassment, she burst out laughing. "I need to get back in the shower. You had chili oil on your fingers. My vagina isn't up to spicy foods." With a gasping laugh, she rushed out of the kitchen to the bathroom.

Anthea followed, making horrified sounds. "I don't believe it. That must hurt like hell. Will the shower help?"

Shay sighed with relief as she bathed her tender flesh with cool water. She sat down in the spray. "How can I fill the tub instead of shower?"

Anthea flipped a lever on the spigot. She sat on the edge of the tub as it filled. "Is there anything I can do?"

"Wash your hands," Shay said. She could smile now that the burning sensation was subsiding.

"I did that before I finished making breakfast. But I should have before I. . . ." Anthea blushed red again.

Shay turned the water off and relaxed for a minute. "You sure do know how to show a girl a hot time."

"Please stop," Anthea said. She hid her face. "This is mortifying. I've never done anything like that in the kitchen and look what happened!"

Shay pondered Anthea's remark. Maybe Anthea wasn't as experienced as she had seemed. Maybe she was just damned good in bed. Or they were just good together. Shay was pleased that no other lover had been with Anthea in the kitchen. Maybe there were other rooms they could inaugurate as well. "If we practice good kitchen hygiene in the future we shouldn't have this problem."

Anthea peered through her hands. "Future? You mean you might forgive me for being so stupid?"

"Forgive you?" Shay stood up and started the

water draining out of the tub. She drew a towel around her hips. "The effects of the chilies are all gone and I'm still on fire." She swallowed, her tongue suddenly thick, her throat tight. She stepped out of the tub. "Take me back to bed."

Anthea's lower lip trembled but she stood up without comment and led Shay back to the bed.

Out of concern for hygiene in a food preparation area, Shay took another shower before leaving for work. Every inch of her body felt covered with Anthea's scent and desire. Since her blouse — recovered from the garden below the deck — was dirty, she borrowed a few items of clothing from Anthea to save the time of going home again . . . a T-shirt, panties, thin socks for her loafers. They were all too big, but they were scented with Anthea. She was fifteen minutes late to work. As if she cared.

Anthea leaned against the wall outside the pizza parlor and watched yet another pair of teenagers in corsets and garters walk by. Things had changed since the last time Anthea had gone to see the *Rocky Horror Picture Show*. It had been playing at the theater across the street every Saturday night for a very long time. She hadn't realized that now kids went to see it half-naked.

She felt a little anxious waiting for Shay like this. They hadn't exactly made plans for her to meet her after work, but Anthea couldn't help herself.

181

Shay finally emerged from the darkened restaurant. She looked tired, but when she saw Anthea waiting for her she looked pleased.

Anthea glanced across the street and had an inspiration. "I was wondering if you'd like to take in a movie."

"*Rocky Horror*? I haven't been in ages," Shay said. "I reek of pizza."

Anthea leaned closer. "I never noticed before, but pizza is pretty sexy."

"Flatterer." Shay glanced over her shoulder, then pulled Anthea into the shadow of the pizzeria doorway. Anthea returned Shay's fierce kiss, her hips pressing Shay against the door.

When Shay finally released her, Anthea took a deep breath to clear her head. "What was I saying?"

"Movie," Shay said. "You don't really want to go to a movie, do you?" One hand slipped up the front of Anthea's sweater.

Anthea shivered. Shay stepped closer to Anthea, brushed an imaginary hair from Anthea's face. Anthea shook her head.

"My apartment's not very far, you know."

"Yes, I know."

Shay turned and Anthea fell into step next to her. Once they were away from the main drag, Shay took Anthea's hand and they walked comfortably together.

At the door, Shay fumbled for her keys. "Let me get the light," she said, going ahead of Anthea.

"No, don't get the light," Anthea said softly. "Take me to bed, Shay. We don't need light there."

Shay groaned, low and powerful, and reached for Anthea. She fit perfectly into the crook of Shay's arm. Shay kissed her gently and held her. Anthea, once they were down on the bed, silently sent thanks to the secretary in the Car Pool Services department who had written *Anthea Rossignole* on a form and sent it to Shay.

Anthea caressed the side of Shay's face, wishing for more kisses, kisses gentle and sweet. This was so slow and soft.

Shay brought the palm of her hand up against Anthea's wetness. Anthea surged against it.

"Yes, let me," Shay murmured against her breast.

Anthea answered with a gasp. Tears weren't far away. She moved harder against Shay's palm, inviting Shay to enter again.

Later, with a long sigh of pleasure, Anthea dissolved under Shay into a languid, satisfied puddle of fulfillment. "That was very nice."

"Mmm." Shay nodded, suddenly sleepy. It was going to be cramped in her narrow bed, but she could manage if Anthea could. She was nearly asleep when Anthea adjusted her position, cushioning Shay's cheek against one breast.

"It's not hard to believe," Shay mumbled.

"Believe what?"

"That you're made up of the dust of exploded stars."

"I'm what?"

"Your body, your skin, your mouth — it's all from the dust of exploded stars." Shay lazily stroked Anthea's stomach. "That's why it's magic under my fingertips. One beautiful double helix spiral after

183

another. . . ." If she said more she didn't remember it the next morning.

Anthea tried to wish away the pain in her neck. She told herself she was dreaming about it being cramped. But it was too late. She could hear Shay's steady breathing just below her chin.

She didn't want to move, but as soon as she told herself she could stay still a little longer, she was of course seized by an overwhelming need to stretch. She tried one leg at a time, but within a few moments Shay was awake.

"Good morning," Anthea said.

Shay's answer was an unhappy groan.

Anthea moved slowly away from Shay. Their skin peeled apart. She limped her way to the bathroom, her hip having fallen asleep during the motionless night. She didn't want to take a shower quite yet, but she did brush her teeth with her finger and some of Shay's toothpaste. Packing a toothbrush and fresh underwear in her purse would have been a smart idea, but she hadn't been thinking about anything but going to bed with Shay.

When she left the bathroom she heard noise from the only other room of Shay's apartment — running water, then the clank of a teakettle being set on a burner. She surveyed the apartment for the first time.

It wasn't any bigger than a dorm room. The bed was elevated off the floor by virtue of four cinder blocks. They were lucky they hadn't knocked the bed off the blocks at one of the more energetic climaxes of the prior night. Anthea shuddered as she recalled Shay's fingers in her — it had felt so good she hadn't been able to breathe.

The rest of the wall space was occupied by boxes of books and bound paperwork. She could see a lot of the titles, and most were along the lines of *Thermodynamics Theory and Statigraphy* and *Hydroponics in Southeast Asia*. She smiled as she spotted a *Star Trek* novel half-hidden under the bed with a stack of Joanna Russ titles not far away. Shay's only chair was layered in cast-off jeans and T-shirts. A pile of library books was heaped near the door. She peeked out of the window. It was early.

When Shay emerged from the microscopic kitchen, Anthea said, "Spend the day with me."

"Okay," Shay said easily. "Would you like a T-shirt to wear while we have tea at the table?"

"Not particularly." Anthea glanced around. "What table?"

Shay laughed. "The same one you ate at last night."

Anthea blushed and dove back onto the bed. "I'll wait here."

They drank tea poured from an antique teapot into small delicate teacups. "My mother's," Shay explained in response to Anthea's admiring stroke of the dragon pattern on the pot. "It went around the world with me and my Dad and so far only one broken cup. I wouldn't have sold it for anything."

Anthea sipped the delicate jasmine tea. She felt decidedly gypsy-ish, sitting cross-legged and stark naked. Yesterday morning she had felt shy, but this morning was different. She was comfortable in Shay's presence, and liked the sensation. As she watched

Shay sip her tea, goose pimples flushed her arms and breasts. It was as if she could feel those fingers inside her again.

"What shall we do today?"

Shay's question broke the languid spell Shay's body was casting over Anthea. "Whatever you like. I exist to serve thee." Anthea accompanied her words with a bow of her head.

"Mmm." Shay wiggled her eyebrows. "Sounds delightful."

Anthea sputtered into her tea, then attempted a seductive smile. "Anything you wish."

"Maybe we'll never go outside," Shay said. They set their cups down and Anthea slowly uncrossed her legs as Shay leaned back against the wall at the head of the bed. Anthea moved slowly toward the invitation. "No darkness or covers this time," Shay said. "I want to watch you."

Anthea lowered her head slowly and brushed her lips against the firm, smooth skin of Shay's thighs. She left small patches of moisture behind and was rewarded by a trembling in one thigh and a low sigh from Shay.

Anthea felt a powerful swell of control. She glanced up and saw that Shay was watching her, but her eyes were unfocused. Tenderly, letting Shay enjoy the anticipation, she dipped her tongue into the beckoning triangle between Shay's legs. She willed herself to taste slowly. Shay's thighs convulsively tried to snap together, but Anthea held them apart, moving faster now and then deeper, savoring the heady taste. Sweet wetness was flowing over her lips and her cheeks as if she were crushing a ripe peach to her mouth. She was drunk on nectar and the sound of Shay's ecstatic, breathless calls.

Shay smiled reassuringly at Anthea as she rang Mrs. Giordano's bell.

"Are you sure I look okay?" Anthea anxiously brushed her hair back over her shoulders.

Shay thought Anthea looked scrumptious, but if she said so they'd go back downstairs and not come out for another three hours. She was ravenous and needed some food before going back to bed. "You look fine."

Anthea looked skeptical.

"I brought an extra pair of hands," Shay told her friend when she opened the door. "Unlike me, she knows how to cook."

Mrs. Giordano looked from Shay to Anthea and smiled. "Isn't this lovely, up so early for a date. Come in, come in. I made a nice coffee cake first thing."

After two large slices of coffee cake, Shay set herself to doing her usual task, laboriously chopping vegetables. She directed Anthea to the coffee grinder. Mrs. Giordano went back to stirring the sauces simmering on the stove top and chatting with Anthea. Well, *chatting* was a nice word for the interrogation Anthea was being put through. How long had she been working? Did she have a degree? And what had her parents done? Did she have any brothers or sisters? Had she voted in the last election?

Anthea seemed to be taking it in good temper,

but then she was just an all-around nice person. She didn't stop her cheerful answers even as she bumped Shay away from the cutting board and deprived her of the knife. Shay watched in amazement as Anthea rapidly sliced the carrots Shay had been wrestling with. She diced two onions in a quarter of the time it would have taken Shay — so quickly, there were no onion tears. Even Mrs. Giordano noticed as the knife made a rapid tattoo on the cutting board. Shay felt a surge of pride as Mrs. Giordano invited Anthea to taste one of the sauces. It had taken Shay three weeks to reach the taster stage.

"A dash more lemon," Anthea said. "At least, I would add more."

Mrs. Giordano tasted and nodded. "You're right, it needs a bit more zip."

They stayed several hours, sampling all the dishes and gobbling down the coffee cake, chopping more vegetables and washing dishes. Anthea didn't seem to mind at all. She was all smiles when Mrs. Giordano invited her to drop by anytime.

Back in Shay's apartment Anthea said, "She needs a Cuisinart and an industrial oven."

"And double the social security income, and a new back," Shay added. "But she gets by with what she has."

Anthea murmured in a distracted tone.

"Hey," Shay said. "You haven't kissed me for three whole hours."

Anthea turned to her, all distraction gone. "Step into my parlor," she said, beckoning as she moved toward the bed.

* * * * *

It was late in the afternoon when Anthea rolled over and said, "When are you going to do that soil sample?"

"What soil . . . oh. I'd forgotten." Shay grimaced and sat up. "What made you think of it?" Shay wondered how Anthea could think after the marathon they'd been through.

"Well, you're going to need some results pretty quickly, aren't you? Why not hop down to the refinery today and get it?"

Shay blinked. "It's a little more complicated than driving up to the well."

Anthea rolled her eyes. "I know we have to stop and get Tyvek suits from somewhere. I've got a cooler we can hold the sample in."

Shay looked at Anthea incredulously. "How did you learn to do a well sample?"

Anthea sat up, looking put out. "For your information, I'm a cost accountant. Procedurally, there's not very much that happens on that refinery that I don't know about. That's how I do my job."

"I didn't mean to impugn your honor," Shay said. She had obviously hit a sore spot. "I had no idea your job required you to get into such detail."

"I know a little bit about everything," Anthea said, apparently mollified.

"You should go on *Jeopardy*. Category: Sampling Devices. Tap water and a plastic wading pool." She nudged Anthea with her knee.

Anthea made a buzzing sound, then said, "What is a portable non-potable decontamination site, Alex."

189

"That's correct so you must be kissed."

"Why, Mr. Trebek," Anthea said. She seized Shay by the shoulders and kissed her fiercely. "How you do talk."

"Didn't you know you were playing for kisses?" Shay's hand drifted to Anthea's breast.

"Stop that," Anthea said. "You're deliberately trying to distract me. What about that sample?"

Shay sighed. "I'd like to keep reality away for a while longer."

Anthea smiled softly and trailed her fingers across Shay's shoulder. "Isn't this real?"

Shay shook her head. "It's too good to be real."

Anthea's smile faded and she said seriously, "What can I do to make it real?"

Shay gulped. "I'm not ready . . . to answer that."

Anthea looked away, chewing her lower lip. "I'm not either. You're the best friend I've had in a while. Can we go on being friends?"

"Just friends?" Shay stroked the side of Anthea's breast.

Anthea shivered and then smiled with what looked to Shay like false bravado. "How about friends who like to screw the daylights out of each other?"

Shay laughed. "I can live with that definition for now."

Anthea nodded. "For now," she echoed softly.

"Well," Shay said. "Since you are determined, how about we go get that sample?"

"Wouldn't waiting until dusk be better? We could get on the premises right as they're turning on the lights. Maybe no one will notice a car in the pipe fields."

"We should probably pick up a vehicle at the trailer. When we get the suits. Much later. To tell you the truth, I need a nap." Shay settled into the corner and pulled Anthea against her.

Anthea showed her badge to the guard at the gate . . . not the regular guy who would have let her go in with a wave. She felt her heart rate go up as she allowed herself to recognize that what they were doing was expressly against company policy. *I could get fired for this.* Entering the premises when not scheduled to work was a "serious" offense. Shay leaned over so the guard could see her badge too.

"I left some baseball tickets in my desk," Anthea said. "At least I think so."

Shay said, "I still say they're in my desk. We're going to have to drive all the way out to the field trailers."

The guard raised the barrier with a toothy smile. "I hope you ladies don't have to spend your night crawling all over this place."

Anthea smiled back and drove slowly ahead.

"He didn't make us sign in," Shay said in a whisper.

Anthea smirked. "Show enough cleavage and you can go anywhere." She glanced down at her light cotton shirt left unbuttoned over a low cut tank top she'd pulled even lower.

"Will you pull that back up, please? I honestly didn't think it would work."

"You can't overestimate a man's ability to underestimate a woman with boobs," Anthea said. "I think Marilyn Monroe or Mae West said that. Or Madonna." Anthea steered them into the empty parking lot right next to the Executive Building.

"Why are we stopping here?"

"Because we're in sight of the Guard station. We'll have to go in." Anthea could feel time ticking away. Would the guard wonder what had kept them? Would he call ahead to other gates asking if they'd left?

She unlocked the main door and Shay followed her inside. Without thinking she summoned the elevator.

"Where are we going?" Shay sounded as impatient as Anthea felt.

"Just killing some time."

"Oh, yeah?" The elevator doors closed and Shay reached over to trace the rim of Anthea's tank top. "I can think of a way or two."

Anthea pushed Shay's hand away. "Stop that, not here. We've got business to attend to." But she could feel herself smiling. Shay planted a kiss right in Anthea's cleavage. "Oh, fie," she whispered. "How can I resist such wiles?"

Shay let her go as the elevator stopped. The doors opened and Anthea pressed for the ground floor.

As the doors closed again, Anthea said, "Now, where were you?"

Anthea had retucked her shirt by the time they returned to the car and she drove with deliberate care out to Shay's work site. Shay let them in and rounded up two Tyvek suits and breathers. When Anthea saw the truck they were heading for she said, "At least this time I'm appropriately attired."

"I must say you're the hottest thing in a Tyvek suit I've ever seen."

"Stop joking," Anthea said. "Right about now this seems like a lot more than a fraternity prank."

"What's the worst that can happen?" Shay unlocked the truck and Anthea scrambled into the passenger seat.

"Oh, they can fire us. You're resigned to that and I guess I'd get over it." Anthea couldn't believe what she was saying. A few months ago she would have said her job was her whole identity. "But we're about to remove something that belongs to the company. They could call the cops." Her mind wrote the headline: LESBIANS CAUGHT STEALING FROM CORPORATE GIANT.

"I'd say two ounces of dirt is petty at most."

Anthea realized her hands had started shaking. "And a sample bottle. I guess it's not grand theft." *No, it's not. Get over it.*

"Hey," Shay said. "If you're having second thoughts, let's not do it."

Anthea shook her head. "No. It has to be done. I can handle it."

Anthea listened carefully while Shay explained the procedures. The sun was dropping behind the foothills between the bay and the ocean. The pipe fields reflected in orange ... it was almost like modern sculpture. As the gloom deepened, some vapor lights snapped on and erased the illusion of art. She could plainly see the grimy metal and barren soil.

"Mask," Shay said. She stopped the truck long enough to pull her breather over her face and ensure that Anthea's was also fitted properly. Anthea's stomach did a slow roll as they passed a sign reading, "Restricted Area — Hazardous Substances."

In the mixed natural and artificial light it seemed unreal to watch Shay standing out on the edge of a thin plank of wood. Anthea waited with the cooler and nervously looked around. *No place to run to, nowhere to hide.* She hummed the tune under her breath to pass the waiting time, then sighed with relief as Shay got to her feet. She sealed the vial, labeled it with an indelible marker, then handed it to Anthea, who dropped it into a Mason jar, snapped the lip closed and put the whole thing in her small cooler. She followed Shay back to the truck, then mimicked her motions at the decontamination stop.

Her heart was pounding. She knew she'd just done something that had changed her life, an act she would have been incapable of a short time ago. Ever since Lois had left, her certainties had come unraveled. She'd thought she'd go back to being the Anthea she was before Lois. It hadn't worked out that way.

She wanted to tell Shay to stop the truck. She wanted to feel Shay's fingers in her, she wanted to bite Shay's nipples. As if they were live wired, Shay would quiver in response. *Maybe this is an automobile fetish I'm developing.* She told herself to get a grip. Now was not the time.

She had thought that discovering her lesbianism

was the biggest change she'd ever go through in her life. Who would have thought she'd have had to wait until her mid-thirties to discover that she was . . . could be . . . passionate. She'd spent years of her life confusing self-control, and self-denial, with purpose.

She followed Shay back into the field trailer. The changes in her life weren't Shay's doing, they were hers and hers alone.

Shay tossed the used suits and breathers into the decontamination bin. She went back to her cube for her fanny pack while Anthea went to the ladies room. She walked toward the bathrooms as she snapped the strap around her waist. Glancing up she saw Anthea opening the door directly ahead. And then someone stepped out of the side hallway between them.

Shay's heart stopped. She felt herself flush with guilt. "Scott, you scared the shit out of me."

"What the hell are you doing here?" Shay decided he didn't sound hostile, just confused.

"I left tickets to the A's game in my desk." She saw Anthea hesitating in the bathroom doorway. "We had to drive all the way down here to get them and we've missed half the game. But there's a great fireworks exhibition."

"Oh —"

"Sorry I took so long," Anthea said. Shay took guilty pleasure in watching Scott jump. "You know what Prince Charles says, never pass a bathroom." Anthea held out her hand to Scott as if their meeting was an everyday business occurrence. "Hi," she said, her voice dripping with charm and good humor, "Anthea Rossignole from costing."

Shay remembered that charm from that safety meeting where they'd first met. It seemed ages ago when she had disliked Anthea for this very same ability to turn on the charm. It was certainly useful now.

"Oh, that's right. I knew I recognized you." Scott slowly looked Anthea up and down and Shay saw her flush slightly.

"Well," Anthea said brightly. "Let's get to the game. The beer's not getting any colder." She swung the cooler she carried.

God, she was calm, Shay thought. "Yeah, let's go," she said. "See you on Tuesday, Scott."

"You two ladies have a great evening."

"What the hell was he doing there?" Anthea kept her tone to a whisper even though they were back in the car.

"I don't know. If he'd been five minutes earlier he'd have seen the suits."

Anthea's flush had deepened. "He looked at me like he couldn't figure out why ... what my excuse was."

"Excuse?" Shay was confused.

"Excuse for being a sexual deviant."

"You're imagining things."

"No, I'm not," Anthea said. Her voice sounded as if her throat were constricted. "I've been stared at. That wasn't just 'hey, honey, I got what you want.' That look said, "one night with me could make you forget her.'" Anthea pursed her lips. "It's been a long time since I've received one. Which way?"

Shay said, "Left, then right." They waited for a hauling truck to amble across the intersection, heading toward the heavy vehicle garage. Shay stared after it for a moment, then cleared her throat. "Does it bother you so much? The way he looked at you?"

"Yes. It bothers me a lot. But . . . the old Anthea would have felt guilty."

Shay gently touched Anthea's shoulder. "And the new Anthea?"

Anthea took a deep, shaky breath. "The new Anthea is pissed. The new Anthea would like to . . . to do something that makes him sorry. I was going to say punch his lights out, but that would violate my nonviolence policy."

Shay laughed. "So when do I meet this new Anthea?" She leaned over with Anthea to wave at the guard. He raised the barrier and returned their wave.

"You had sex with her in her kitchen."

"Oh, so that's the new Anthea. I liked her a lot." The refinery was fading behind them and Shay felt lightheaded. "Oh, God. I can't believe we pulled it off. I feel like Thelma and Louise."

"Neither can I," Anthea said. "It makes me feel. . . ."

"What?"

Anthea glanced over at Shay, her lips slightly parted, eyes shining. "Like I . . . like I want to. . . ."

Shay stroked Anthea's hand. "Take me to your place."

Anthea looked over at her. "You want to?"

"God, Andy. I want —" Shay licked her lips. Her throat was suddenly parched.

"Want what?" Anthea's voice was a whispering caress.

"I want tonight to make the last two days look like amateur practice. Next time you touch me I want you to do it for hours."

9
Dead End

Shay could feel Harold staring at her — he'd been doing it all morning. She found herself repeatedly fighting a blush. How could he possibly know, she asked herself. He nonchalantly suggested they have lunch together and it wasn't until they were facing each other across the cafeteria table that he said something.

"So?"

"So what?" Shay took a bite of her peanut butter

and jelly and thought longingly of the crepes Anthea had dished out for lunch the day before, and the hot dogs and nachos they had eaten after Anthea treated them to the July 4th baseball game. Just so they could honestly both say they'd been to a ball game.

Harold swallowed another forkful of salad and chewed thoughtfully. "I guess nothing happened, then."

"I don't know what you're talking about," Shay said. She immediately knew she'd played too innocent because Harold grinned knowingly.

"That's right, there aren't any roses in those cheeks or stars in those eyes. You're not walking around about three feet off the floor."

"I'm just trying to duck Scott, that's all."

Harold gave a hoot of laughter. "And that sunburn on your nose doesn't mean you were up to anything either."

Shay put her hand to her nose. "I went to a ball game."

"And . . . ?"

"And none of your business."

"Aw-right, she got lucky." Harold munched on his salad with a triumphant air. "It's nice to know you've got a life."

"Look, I can do without the teasing," Shay said. "I'm not ready for it."

"Did you really think that just because we're buds I wouldn't tease you?"

"It's what I was dreading." She sipped her soda, feeling sulky.

Harold just smiled innocently and concentrated on his salad. After a few minutes he said, "Why are you avoiding Scott?"

"Because I need to confront him about something and then I guess I'll be looking for work." She didn't mention the sample Anthea was taking to a lab during her lunch hour. The results wouldn't be available until next week. "I want to put it off for about a week."

Harold looked concerned as he put down his fork. "I'll be supportive first. I'm very sorry to hear you are having problems and support you in your efforts to work them out." He sighed. "Now I'll be selfish. What the fuck am I supposed to do if you leave?"

It was her turn to sigh. "I don't know. But I'm pretty sure it's inevitable."

"Damn. Just when I was looking forward to work again."

"Sorry, Harold. I did introduce you to a new guy, though, one who works here."

"Yeah, a guy I have a date with this Friday night. I guess that helps a little. Are you sure you have to do this?"

Shay nodded. "Unless I'm completely off the beam about something. I won't know until Friday, maybe Monday."

"You sure do know how to ruin a guy's day."

"Sorry. You can call me peewee if you like." But Harold didn't smile.

By Friday Harold seemed resigned. He alternately referred to her as a traitor and a peewee and made lewd but true comments about how Shay seemed to be running late in the mornings and several days in a row wore shirts several sizes too large. She couldn't tell him that she should be exhausted from the extra exertion — he'd only ask just what she was exerting herself at. How could she explain, without boasting like men she detested, about the endless lovemaking that started as soon as she and Anthea reached the car and ended the next morning when they parted. While she was driving, Anthea had a way of stroking the inside of Shay's knee that made Shay go limp.

She told herself she ought to keep a little distance. She told herself that she had no idea where this affair was going. She told herself that the sex couldn't stay this good.

Friday evening, Anthea drove them to her house.

Shay collapsed onto the sofa with a sigh of relief. "I can't believe how tense I was all week."

"I kept expecting my boss to call me into his office," Anthea said, stepping into the bedroom to change. "Want to go to a movie tonight?"

"Let's watch something on the tube," Shay said. "I can't really afford the movies."

"My treat," Anthea called. She pulled a polo shirt over her head, then slipped into jeans. As she headed back to the living room she said, "What do you want to see?" She stopped at the sight of Shay sitting bolt upright, both fists clenched.

"I can't afford to go the movies," she said slowly, her voice tight.

"I'm more than happy to pay," Anthea said again.

"That's not the point."

"Why are you upset?"

Shay hopped to her feet and paced to the French doors. "I don't need to be . . . kept."

Anthea laughed. Shay whirled to face her and Anthea realized she'd done exactly the wrong thing. "I'm sorry. It was just . . . this is kind of unexpected. What's the harm in me paying for the movies?"

"I don't like to be dependent."

"It's not your rent," Anthea said, with a flash of temper. "It's just a lousy movie." Things Lois had said were coming back and she didn't want to discuss them again.

"It doesn't feel right," Shay said, her expression stony.

"This is silly," Anthea said. "My parents left me money. I can spend it any way I like. I'd like to spend some of it on us having fun together."

Shay was shaking her head vehemently. "I can't explain it. I just can't sit and do nothing while you give me things I can't reciprocate." She sank down onto the sofa again.

Anthea choked back a flood of confused anguish. *Nothing?* Too fast . . . they'd gotten here too fast. She'd been falling in love with Shay over a period of five months. Ninety minutes or more, five days a week. It was a long, slow fall, so gentle she hadn't noticed it happening until she'd hit bottom. But it had only taken one week to start fighting about money. "There's more than nothing going on between us," she said finally, looking away.

Shay was silent for so long that Anthea looked back at her. She was astounded to see Shay holding her head in her hands, shoulders shaking silently with tears.

Anthea froze. She couldn't deal with her own

tears, which is why she didn't cry, let alone someone else's. She slowly sat down and pulled Shay gently into her arms. She proffered a clean tissue she found in her pocket, which was accepted, and then she rocked Shay, wondering what nerve she had touched to have crumbled this strong woman so completely.

Shay grew calmer after a few minutes, then mumbled an apology. Anthea continued to rock her until Shay sat up and blew her nose. "I'm sorry," she said again. "I don't know what set me off."

"I didn't mean to be insensitive," Anthea began, but Shay turned to face her.

"It's not you. Well, it's only a little bit you. I . . . I realized how much I feel like a nothing. No hopes, no dreams, no plans, no prospects." She drew a shuddering breath, then caught Anthea's hand, which was stroking her arm, and held it in her lap. "Everything I ever planned to be was wrapped up in my dad. I don't know why he died. I still get so mad at him."

"It's okay," Anthea said. "It's okay to be mad."

Shay blew her nose again. "I can't believe, after all I wanted to do with my life, that I'm spinning my wheels at a place which is everything I wanted to change. I . . . I'm still empty inside. There's a big hole he left. I could fill it up with you but that wouldn't be right."

"Shay," Anthea said softly, "tell me."

"There's something I don't usually think a lot about, but it's been coming to me lately, like a bitter pill about something old. I . . . my dad's brothers offered to pay for the funeral, but it would have had to be their way and Dad didn't want to be buried in the family plot. And they hadn't talked in decades because my dad wouldn't join in on a lawsuit to get compensation for the property the government took when my grandparents were interned."

"Interned?" Anthea echoed the word uncertainly. "You mean in World War Two?"

Shay got up and moved to the glass doors. Fading sunlight painted the ceiling orange. She nodded. "They owned a bookstore which was foreclosed on because they weren't making their payments. They weren't making their payments because they were in a camp. The store was sold for nothing to white people in the government. They held onto the land for about five years, then sold it for a half a million dollars to a white developer. The developer sold it to another white man for double that, and right now that land is a piece of what's holding up the Bonaventure Hotel in downtown Los Angeles." She cleared her throat. "I agree completely with my uncles that our family — lots of families — lost futures that are beyond price and they lost them to the benefit of many white people who just happened to be some of the same white people who decided to have all the slant-eyed Americans put in a camp."

Anthea said nothing. What could she say that would make up for the past?

"Letting it bother me doesn't do any good. My dad didn't like looking back. I really don't either, so I don't know why this bothers me now. He was the baby of the family. He didn't really remember the camp. He lived without its shadow and he never knew what his older brothers lost. I never thought about what wealthy grandparents might have meant in my life, at least not until I met you. That I might have met you as an equal."

Anthea felt a chill run down her arms. "We are equals."

"Easy for you to say," Shay said with a sigh. "If you had nothing but burdens and debts and I had money, would you let me pay for everything?"

"I'd work to the best of my ability. I'd try to be the best person you could love. If I did that I might feel equal," Anthea said. She hugged her knees, hoping to soothe the ache in the pit of her stomach.

"That's part of the problem, don't you see?" Shay fixed Anthea with an imploring gaze. "I can't even work to the best of my ability. I hate everything NOC-U stands for. I can't tell if I'm in love with you or I'm just looking for a way to get out of there. Suddenly I see how comfortable life can be — me, the daughter of a man who spent his life wholeheartedly believing that having money corrupts people." Shay turned away. With the light behind her she glowed in an outline of old gold, but her face was steeped in shadow. "Money's like fire. It's just a tool. It's how you use it that makes all the difference. My dad was afraid of it. And all I know is my career has crumbled because he's gone and I don't know if what I feel for you is something . . . special . . . or if I'm hoping to make you my career."

Anthea couldn't help her wooden tone. "I don't think I'd like you if you did."

"I wouldn't like me. I'm sorry I was so touchy about going to the movies. It's not what bothers me. I'm afraid I'm mercenary." She finished with a little hiccup.

Anthea was at a loss for words. She groped for a

way to express herself. "I could promise to never give you another thing ever, but I know I'd break it. If money's a tool, then let me use it to make our times together memorable."

Shay said quietly, "I'm afraid to count on it."

Anthea got up and joined her at the window. She took one of Shay's hands in her own. "You can count on it. You can count on me." She wanted to remove all their clothes and press their bodies together so they could be just two women, loving each other, beyond race and history and bank accounts. She pulled gently and Shay moved into her arms.

Early Monday morning Shay's desk phone rang and Anthea said breathlessly, "I have the data, but I don't know what it means."

"Tell me," Shay said. She poised her pencil and wrote the number Anthea gave her on her blotter. She outlined it as her head began to spin. "Maybe I'm not out of a job after all," she said in a low voice. "It looks like you wasted your money. That result is marginally less than the prior quarter and a lot less than this quarter's . . . the sample I thought was right."

"What does it mean?"

"It means I don't know what I'm doing. I'm sorry. Let's talk about it later, okay?"

"Sure." Anthea's tone changed. "See you tonight."

"Right," Shay said with as much enthusiasm as she could gather. She put the receiver down distractedly.

Harold leaned back in his chair. "Sorry to

eavesdrop, as if I could avoid it. I take it you won't be doing whatever it is you thought you'd have to do?"

Shay shook her head. "I was so sure I was right. . . ." She reached into her desk drawer to pull out her file set of the original test results — the results that showed the xylene level shooting up in the last quarter. For a moment she stared at two nearly identical reports then realized that one of the copies was the set of data that had nothing to do with NOC-U. NEM, Inc.'s results, whatever NEM stood for. She should throw it away because it was too similar to her own data and she didn't want to make a mistake. Aside from the data, the reports were identical, right down to the well labels.

Right down to the well labels.

Inexplicably her hands began to shake. When she'd first seen the data for NEM, Inc., she had been bothered by something and now she realized what it was. Two different companies were using identical yet highly esoteric well labels. The NEM sampling date was seven days before her own data's sampling date. She scanned the numbers. In three of the forty well results, the NEM report was significantly higher than the NOC-U report.

The three wells that were different included the one she had resampled with Anthea. The data for NEM, Inc.'s well B-B-146 was higher than the data for NOC-U's well B-B-146. With well labels like that, how easy it would be to get confused, Shay thought. How easy it would be to mislead yourself or others about the data. The higher NOC-U data was being dismissed by Scott as a lab error. Well, one of them was wrong . . . or was it?

Even more confusing was that the test Anthea had paid for had shown a result less than either of the other two reports. There was a piece of the puzzle missing, something that refused to make sense. After all, what the data told her, if all the samples were accurate, was that in a matter of a quarter the xylene level at B-B-146 jumped impossibly, then reduced over time to a level below its previous quarter. It was highly improbable.

Her temples were pounding as she tried to make the leap of logic necessary to make sense of three sets of results — she was convinced that the NEM report was really NOC-U data — taken within weeks on the same well giving three significantly different xylene levels. The most recent result, the one Anthea had paid for, was the only one at an acceptable level.

"Earth to Shay."

She realized with a start that Harold had been talking to her. "I need to talk to you," she told him. "But not here. And it's urgent."

Harold studied her face for a minute, then glanced at the data sheets she was clutching. "What's up?"

"Not here."

"Then where?"

"Lunch."

Anthea changed lanes and then shook her head at Shay. "I'm so confused. Start over."

"Okay. Sample one was taken by me for NOC-U last quarter. Let's call it the baseline. Sample two was taken by NEM about eleven weeks later. Compared to sample one, it shows a dramatic increase in xylene. Sample three was taken by me for NOC-U one week after that, and its result is more than the baseline, but less than sample two. And sample four, the one you and I took, is lower than the baseline."

"That doesn't make sense." Anthea's mental video dropped the scenario onto a line chart and the ups and downs just weren't computing.

"Harold, with his devious mind, came up with a scenario that does cover most of the situation, but it's really wild. However, it could be right. He got the idea because of a change in soil composition he found in his sample work. Our work is divided up between constituent analysis — that's me — and soil content analysis, which is Harold's specialty."

"Content analysis?"

"How much clay, how much sand, how much of certain minerals. All the refinery soil is pretty clayey, though because of dredging and the tectonic plate, there's a lot of gravelly clay and clayey gravel."

"Uh-huh." Anthea tried to look like she understood.

"Anyway, his soil content shifted. Not dramatically, but he has more clay than in the past and nothing to account for it. He really was going to consider it sampling error — there was no reason not to. Like I said, he's devious, though."

"I'm ready," Anthea said. She braked for the Dumbarton backup and divided her attention between the traffic and Shay.

"Let's say that on the other side of the refinery

you have a serious xylene leak. Really serious. Bad enough to get your xylene production stopped. If you're a money-sucking corporate capitalist pig, you don't want that to happen. So instead, you keep it quiet and start moving soil. You spread the contaminated soil everywhere. After all, a little xylene everywhere is less detectable than a whole lot in one place."

"So your sample did have xylene in it, but it's from . . . imported soil? It does sound a little wild."

"That's the rational part," Shay said with something between a laugh and a grunt. "Then, because you're a money-sucking corporate capitalist pig, the people you hire to move the soil are basically not too bright. They get confused about where you tell them not to put it. So they put it in places where the soil's being sampled already."

"Hence your xylene suddenly jumping. Okay, this is getting good."

"You get wind of the screw up and take some samples to see how bad the damage is. And because you're a money-sucking —"

"I get the point —"

"— you take them to the same low bidder lab that does all your testing and just put them under a slightly different name. And then some smartass like me sees the data and finally notices that the well labels are identical."

"I'm lost."

"You're so lazy you don't even relabel the wells for your own use. So I saw a duplicate soil analysis report for the other company. I have it right here. If I had invoices for the work to move the soil, I'd have a case for the EPA."

"But why did the xylene level go down for our sample?"

"Oh, I left out the best part. After the company gets their own private sample results, they realize the xylene jump is going to show up on the reports to the Water Board. So you do an emergency remediation. Haul out the contaminated soil and put clean in its place, water the entire area like hell and hope for the best. It has some effect . . . my sample was up, but not up as high as their private sample. And our sample was even lower."

"If this all happened, it was really expensive."

"As expensive as closing down xylene production? For seven to ten years?"

Anthea chewed on the inside of her cheek for a moment. "No."

Anthea assumed a nonchalant air and strolled across the floor to the product accounting group. After discussing it well into the night with Shay, they had decided she was the one to get the hauling invoices . . . if they existed. And she knew who she could ask.

Ruben was happy to see her — it showed in his face. "I'm glad I'm back here, but I'd rather work for you," he told her in a confidential whisper. "You like to teach and here I already know what I'm doing." He shrugged one shoulder.

"Next opening I have I'll see if I can get a transfer for you," Anthea said sincerely. "The work keeps piling up so sooner or later I'll have to hire someone. And I'm not just saying that because I need a favor."

"Okay, shoot," Ruben said.

"Well, I have a problem with a cost study and I want to check the work we did. But I don't want to broadcast to the whole company that I'm reexamining a study. The product managers get hysterical."

Ruben rolled his eyes. "Tell me about it."

"So I was wondering if I gave you an array of account numbers, if you could print some invoices for me off the microfiche."

He pushed a paper and pencil at her. "Just make a list. I'll do it when I'm finished with the current project. Maybe Thursday."

"You're a savior," Anthea said. She started writing.

Anthea handed the envelope of invoices to Shay as she settled into the car on Thursday afternoon. "I didn't dare look. I don't think I'm cut out for cloak-and-dagger work."

"You've been doing great," Shay said. She wanted to kiss the worried frown from Anthea's mouth. Instead she kissed her finger and pressed it to the back of Anthea's hand. Oh my, she thought, she really shouldn't look at those hands if she wanted to keep her mind on the invoices. If men have to wear pants, then lesbians should have to wear mittens.

Once they were out on the freeway, Shay began sorting the invoices. "What is all this stuff?"

"Oh, I had to give Ruben a range of account codes so the one I wanted didn't stand out. And Adrian, who has no idea why I made it such a priority all of a sudden, finished compiling GPG's cost data. You all have done a great deal of hauling and used an amazing number of outside contractors."

"You're kidding. They didn't even charge it to a product?"

Anthea shook her head. "I checked the xylene production costs . . . no hauling there."

Shay made a rude sound with her lips. "The assholes. They couldn't resist the chance to jack up the cost of the Groundwater Protection Grid so they can scream about how much the existing remediation order costs." She continued to thumb through the invoices.

Anthea said quietly, "Have you given any thought to who 'they' are?"

Shay had, but she didn't know enough about the corporate set-up to guess. "It has to be somebody high up enough to authorize the expense without alerting too many people."

"A senior veep or higher. Pretty darned high."

Shay looked up at Anthea. "You're afraid you're going to get caught, aren't you?"

Anthea nodded, but she was smiling. "I have this problem with authority. Even if they are money-sucking capitalist pigs, I want them to like me."

Shay laughed. "Well, I hope it won't come to that. And I hope I'm not being naive." They drove in silence as Shay worked. Once she figured out the coding, the invoices she was interested in were easy to spot.

"Here's one. Holy moly, it's got the refinery grid numbers, volume of soil and the starting and ending times, and the date. Hah! Moving soil at three in the morning is not standard operating procedure. If we can get some refinery maps that have marked grids we'll be able to draw it out."

"I take it that's good."

"I think so," Shay said. "Good enough to make the EPA very, very interested." Her palms were sweating. She relished the idea of presenting the summary of the entire business to the EPA. All she needed was a favorable ear. Someone like Joan Lewis. And maybe there were a few people in her dad's address book who were still there.

"How are we going to get grid maps?"

"That I don't know," Shay said. "The ones in the trailer are about four foot by six and bound. Making copies would be obvious."

Anthea was silent for a long time. They were past San Leandro when she finally spoke up. "I think Adrian — I could be wrong, but I think he used to go with a guy who worked in graphic arts. We may not be able to get maps, but we might be able to get the files they use for permit applications. Graphics files marked with the grid."

Shay bared her teeth with a big grin. "That would be *perfect*. We can mark up the printouts or print them with the information on them."

215

"It'll definitely look like an inside job," Anthea said. Her worried frown returned. "I can't put Adrian at risk, too."

"I suppose that if we wanted to, we could go to the county engineer's office and pay for maps with grid markings and then have them scanned. But Adrian's friend's files would be much faster."

"I'll ask him about it tomorrow, but he has the right to say no."

Shay left the envelope of invoices on the kitchen counter and helped Anthea make dinner. She felt like a computer that had been given the priority task of solving pi to the last digit; she had no capacity left for thinking of anything but the three well results and the invoices.

It was a reflex that made her stand on tiptoe behind Anthea to kiss her neck. It was something she would naturally do with her lover . . . with the woman she loved.

She jolted into the here and now.

The woman she loved . . . it didn't seem possible. It had taken so long to get to know Anthea even remotely well and even now Shay knew Anthea had depths she hadn't seen. And yet loving her seemed so easy. So easy she wanted to be suspicious of it, like wondering if it was Anthea's secure financial position, not Anthea herself. She knew Anthea thought that they could just agree to put the money aside, but it was about as easy as forgetting Anthea was white. It had an impact on their relationship and she should be on guard against feeling anything for the money.

Perhaps her success in discovering NOC-U's illegal toxic dumping was pumping up her self-esteem because the question was bothering her less. But it still nagged at her.

Forget about your pride, she told herself, what about your heart? The woman she loved had an exquisite neck, for example. Up on her tiptoes, she kissed it again.

"What's that for?" Anthea wiggled her rear end, which distracted Shay a great deal.

It would be very easy to forget pride, heart and independence for the joy of stroking Anthea's velvet backside. "I like your house," she said finally. An inane thing to say, she thought, when what she wanted to say was much more serious.

Anthea was cutting zucchini into julienne strips. "Enough to live here?" Her voice sounded nonchalant but there was a break in the steady beat of the knife on the chopping block.

The question was so unexpected that Shay didn't know what to say. She knew how she felt, but was completely in the dark about Anthea's feelings. Except for the sex. It was clear Anthea enjoyed the sex a lot.

Anthea dropped her knife and whirled around. "I'm sorry. I ... I'm not putting any pressure on you or asking you to live with me or anything like that. It's only been a couple of weeks. We should probably date for a while. . . ."

"I wouldn't exactly call it dating. That sounds so . . . civilized," Shay said. You don't make me feel civilized in the least, she thought.

"I feel like I've known you for ages, but really, I don't want to pressure you."

Shay looked anxiously up into Anthea's face. "I'm . . . I'd like . . . Can we not ask that yet? I feel so up in the air. I'll be looking for another job soon and . . . I'm so unsettled I can't think about settling."

"But you might consider it?" The tiny freckles dusting Anthea's cheeks were plainly visible for once.

"I've already considered it." Parts of her mind were telling her it would never work. Anthea was too closeted. Too rich. Too white. Too Yuppified. But she couldn't possibly say anything but yes. Whenever Anthea asked her. If Anthea asked her.

Which meant she was in love.

It felt really, really good.

It scared her to death.

Anthea opened her mouth, then closed it again. There was an uncomfortable silence, then Anthea finally said, "Do you want to make something for dessert?"

Shay smiled, though the feeling of anticlimax was overwhelming. "I thought I could just have you."

"Want to go over to the Cafe Ptomaine with me?"

Adrian looked up at Anthea suspiciously. "Usually you just demand my presence. Why the soft gloves?"

"Oh, no particular reason." Anthea felt a blush start at her neck.

"Are you getting married or something?"

Anthea smiled. "Well, as a matter of fact, I might be getting or-somethinged. But that's not the reason for the lunch invite."

"Just my charming personality, I suppose." Adrian twisted his lips to one side. "Against my better judgment I'll have lunch with you. Are you buying?"

Anthea raised one eyebrow. "Are you kidding? This is the woman who made it possible for you to have dinner with a certain athlete, remember?"

Anthea waited until Adrian was halfway through his plate of cafeteria beef stew — they had the audacity to call it beef bourguignon — before she led the conversation around to the topic of ex-lovers. More explicitly, Adrian's ex-lovers.

"You know the guy I mean. The one who does graphics for engineering —"

"Oh, yeah, Erik. What about him?"

"Do you still keep in touch? I don't know how much people keep in touch with their ex-lovers."

"You haven't kept in touch with any of yours. You probably will never say two words to Lois whereas I talk to Erik all the time."

"Why is that?"

Adrian shrugged. "We made something together. We did some things together for the first time. Don't get that prudish look on your face," he said. "You have a one track mind. Erik and I learned to scuba dive together. We still have it in common."

Anthea munched on a crouton. Had she and Lois made anything together? Or did they just happen to be doing the same things at the same time? She shook the thought away and remembered what she wanted to find out. "So you still talk?"

"Once a month or so," Adrian said. He suddenly

snapped to, a hint of suspicion in his eyes. "What do you want with Erik?"

"Well . . ."

"Oh, God," Adrian said. "You and what's-her-name want to have a baby together and you need a stud."

Anthea clapped a hand over her mouth. She could feel herself blushing. She swallowed and said, "We do not!"

"I don't know why you'd want Erik's genes, anyway. He's got bad knees."

"I need something he may have."

Adrian waited for a second, then said, "Is this twenty questions? Do I have to drag it out of you?"

"I need some maps of the refinery that have grid locators on them."

"You can order a set . . ." Adrian's voice trailed away as Anthea shook her head vehemently.

"No one can know where I got them."

Adrian put down his fork. "You'll have to do better than that."

Anthea dropped her voice. "Shay needs them for a . . . project."

"Some consulting work? But why NOC-U's maps?"

"It's not consulting. There's something going on, something illegal," she whispered. "The maps will help build a case."

Adrian looked skeptical. "A case for what?"

"Keep your voice down," Anthea hissed. "They've been moving soil around that may not be clean."

Adrian leaned toward her. "Why do we care about dirty dirt?"

"Because on an oil refinery, dirty dirt means *toxic*."

Adrian's eyebrows disappeared into his hair. "Are you sure?" His voice ended with a squeak.

Anthea nodded. After sorting the invoices, they had found a handful that were decidedly suspicious — charged to GPG, approval from one senior vice president, work done at night, and involving several cubic tons of soil each. Shay had written down the grid markings and sneaked a quick look at the map book this morning. She'd called to say, cryptically, that the tracks were pretty plain.

"So you think Erik's graphic files will give you the info you need?"

"We need grid markers and general landmarks — just what they use for permit applications. I remembered Erik and —"

"Decided to bribe me with a piece of cafeteria chocolate cake," Adrian said.

Anthea frowned. "What cake?"

Adrian fluttered his eyelashes at her. "Better yet, I've heard for ages about your gourmet kitchen, and there's this athletic-type guy I want to impress, but I can't afford Chez Panisse. . . ."

Anthea tried not to smile. In as severe a tone as she could manage, she said, "Saturday night. At six. Bring the goods and don't be late."

10
Thru Traffic

"You're fussing too much," Shay said.

Anthea looked up as she sliced the last strawberry into the mixed fruit. "It's not fussing. I love to cook. My second favorite way to spend a Saturday." Anthea watched Shay's gaze travel over the various bowls and platters on the kitchen island. She playfully slapped Shay's hand away from the bowl of natillas sauce.

"What's the first way?" Shay sampled some of the diable mushroom filling instead.

Anthea smirked an answer as she stirred the natillas sauce into the fruit. Then she smiled innocently as Shay hurriedly gulped from her glass of iced tea. Diable mushrooms were a specialty.

After clearing her throat, Shay said, "Oh, yes, well, there is that and I must say it was rather fun." Anthea thought she saw the skin on Shay's throat turn a slightly tawnier shade. It had been a memorable send-off before Shay had left for her stint at the pizzeria. Shay cleared her throat again. "That stuff is hot as hell."

"Why, thank you," Anthea said.

"I meant the mushrooms." Shay peered into the other bowls. "And what is this for," she asked, prodding a bowl of soft meringue.

"The fruit sauce and hollandaise only took egg yolks, so I made a meringue from the whites."

"Oh, I see. You were just using up spare ingredients." One cheek dimpled as Shay looked back at Anthea.

"Well, yes. Hollandaise for the salmon, natillas for the fruit, which means a meringue for the gateau ganache. Adrian said that Harold loves chocolate."

Shay smiled fondly at her. "What I see is a salad, fish, some potatoes smothered in cream and cheese, and two desserts. And fried bread."

"That's polenta, not fried bread." Anthea glanced down at her hips. She sighed. "Maybe I should start on an exercise routine."

Shay's expression changed completely — her eyebrows flew up and her mouth opened slightly.

"Oh, no, that's not what I meant. I mean I love watching you enjoy cooking and eating. You obsess about cholesterol and fiber during the week, it's kind of funny that you go so whole hog the other way on the weekend. That's why I trimmed my Saturday shift to five hours — so I could eat you for dinner —" Anthea hooted "— I mean eat *with* you for dinner."

Anthea poured the fruit mix into her glass-lined copper bowl. She twisted open a few slices of orange for garnish, then stood back to study the effect. "I've been thinking I should take up running or something. I gained ten pounds since I quit smoking." After a minor adjustment, she carried the bowl to the refrigerator. The urge for a cigarette came about once a day now. She began snicking small flakes of orange peel onto the salmon.

Shay made a yum-yum noise as she watched the salmon preparations. "That's not a crime. We all can't have Martina's stomach. The washboard stomach is a recent fad, you know. You have a stomach that would have put most painters into a dead faint. It does me."

"You're just saying that." Anthea felt inordinately pleased. She had been certain Shay thought she was fat.

"I didn't fall for an American Gladiator. I suppose if you wanted to turn into She-Ra, Princess of Large Boobs and No Hips, I would support you...." Now Shay was wrinkling her nose.

Anthea laughed and said, "Would you shave the chocolate for me?"

* * * * *

Shay opened the door to Adrian and Harold. At first glance, they were casually attired, but she noted the extra touches that said Serious Male Dressing. Adrian's boots had a blinding shine and Shay could have cut herself on the crease in his black jeans. Harold looked as if he'd been poured into his 501s and black pullover. Something about gay men in San Francisco, she thought. Fashion divas even when they probably aren't trying. Of course, this would be their second date, which might account for the extra care they'd obviously both taken.

Adrian whistled as they crossed the living room. "I work with Andy six years and don't know about this view."

Harold seemed speechless. He silently handed over a bottle of wine.

"Thanks," Shay said.

Harold seemed to find his voice. "Is that a ganache?" he asked Anthea.

"With caramel pecan filling."

"What's a ganache?" Adrian stooped to inspect the chocolate-covered confection.

Harold gave him a pitying look. "It'll be another first for our relationship."

"I had no idea I was dating a gourmet cook."

"I'm simply a gourmet," Harold said. "I don't have much success cooking it, but I do love to eat it."

Adrian made an appreciative noise.

Shay groaned loudly and said, "Let's not start that conversation again. We've already done all the food and eating puns, guys."

"Darn." Adrian leaned on the counter and watched Anthea finish the last touches on the salmon.

Anthea looked up at him. "You brought the maps this meal is buying?"

As Shay took the envelope, Adrian said, "Erik didn't ask what I wanted them for, not after I said he really didn't want to know. These are copies of his printouts as well as diskettes to print more."

Shay started to open the envelope, but Anthea said rather sharply, "After dinner, please. The salmon is not going to share the table with refinery maps."

Shay conceded with a smile and set the envelope aside. "Is it time for those mushroom thingies to come out of the oven?"

Anthea glanced at the clock. Shay had the sudden urge to kiss her all over, she was so adorable when she took charge. "Just about. Why don't you get the pitcher of fire extinguisher out of the lower fridge."

"Fire extinguisher?" Adrian and Harold spoke simultaneously, then looked at each other.

Anthea laughed with an evil touch. "You'll need it with the mushrooms."

Shay didn't know if it was the tingle of the wine or the sparkle of Anthea's best china and crystal, or the soft light dancing off the small chandeliers in the dining room, but she couldn't remember when she'd had so much fun at a meal. It was an odd but pleasant feeling. She thought of her father suddenly, and how for most of her adult life they'd shared almost every meal, sometimes in appalling conditions. It had been just the two of them. Until recently, she'd have given almost anything to go back to that life. But not anymore. The landscape of her world had changed, and with it her perspective on herself. She felt maudlin all of a sudden, as if she should make a note of the time as something slipped away, but she couldn't really say what was disappearing.

"You're all going on so much, but I just love to cook," Anthea was saying. "I just love to and it's nice to have people to cook for." She glanced at Shay with a smile as she brought the fruit bowl to the table, with four crystal bowls.

Shay made a moaning, appreciative sound when she tasted the sauce she'd said was fussing. She'd grown so used to the way food was served in the pizza parlor — plain everything on plain tables. And the special touch of a creamy, sweet sauce on chilled pineapple, strawberries and melon was fussing — and it was worth it.

Anthea said, slowly, "This is going to sound very strange, but this is the first time in my life that I've felt this comfortable in my own home. Until tonight, I felt like I was ... keeping it nice until the real owner came home."

"Maybe that's the fire," Adrian said.

"The fire or the shadow of my parents." Anthea shrugged.

"Oh, no wonder," Harold said. "I kept thinking everything seemed new. I thought you had redecorated, but you rebuilt, didn't you?"

Anthea nodded. "It's roughly the same floor plan, but I did make some improvements. I miss the trees.

We had these big eucalyptus trees — four of them just along the property line. They went up like torches. I watched them explode on the news."

There was a little silence, then Shay said, "Well, on that mortal thought, let's get to work."

Harold said, "What happened to the ganache?"

Anthea smiled wickedly. "I plan ahead. After a couple of hours of playing with our maps we're going to want chocolate."

Anthea felt decidedly unscientific as Shay and Harold punched away at their HP calculators and spoke in a foreign language about velocity heads and permeability boundaries. She and Adrian waded through the invoices and devised a cataloging system to mark the soil movement on the grid as well as the more esoteric symbols for mineral content and groundwater movement. Though they were careful with the maps, they were soon wearing thin from erasing and remarking.

"We're going to need to print out more," Adrian said as his eraser went through the corner of the map that contained well B-B-146.

"What software do we need?"

Adrian dug in the envelope for a diskette. "Never heard of it." He handed it to Anthea.

She grimaced. "It's an illustration program. My computer at work doesn't have the operating system for it, not that I want to be caught dead printing out these maps at work." She thought for a moment, considering the alternatives. "I've always wanted a computer at home," she said. She could lease something, maybe, or just buy it. Something she could make use of after the current project. Something Shay could use, too.

Shay glanced up from the worksheet she and Harold were hunched over. "What computer?"

"We need one that'll run Windows and has a high-resolution video card."

Harold snorted. "Don't look at me. Our dinosaurs at the trailers are two-eighty-sixes."

Adrian made his very-Adrian sound of disgust. "That's cheap. Of course, we're still waiting for requisition approval for our upgrades for last year's releases."

"Andy, I can't let you buy —" Shay began.

"If I were a client, I'd provide you with the equipment, wouldn't I?"

"No, we'd buy the equipment and bill you for the use of it while we worked on your project."

Anthea shrugged. "Same difference. So consider me a client for the purpose of this project. Besides, you're going to need a word processor at a minimum."

Shay was frowning. "I don't like it."

Harold said, "What's not to like? This work needs to be done and there's someone who's willing to pay for it."

Shay's frown intensified. "But I'm sleeping with that someone."

Adrian laughed and said, "So where's the problem?"

Anthea met Shay's gaze. "Let me do this. It matters to me as much as to you."

Anthea could sense Shay's reluctance and confusion as she sighed. "Okay, okay," Shay said.

Anthea smiled brilliantly. Maybe she was finally smoothing down Shay's rough edges about money. "And after that, maybe you could tell me when Mrs. Giordano's birthday is. There's a stove I want to get her."

Shay winced. "I'm losing this battle, aren't 1?"

Adrian glanced at them. "Is there a war?"

Harold stretched. Anthea thought his shirt would burst as the muscles rippled along his shoulders. "So where are we," he said around a half-concealed yawn.

"Time for cappuccino and ganache," Anthea said. She listened to Shay's summary as she set up the machine.

Adrian moaned and said, "I've died and gone to Yuppie heaven."

"Our data is only for the last six months, and the invoices only go back slightly further than that. So the pattern we have is compressed in time. It's hard to show any kind of constituent movement in such a short period, but here's what we have." Anthea glanced up to watch Shay gesture from grid map to grid map. "We start with three wells showing xylene here, here, and here six months ago, at levels approaching the hazardous line. Then, a one-third reduction of xylene in all three wells four months later. Then we use the NEM data to show spikes of xylene suddenly appearing here, here and here. Two of those wells weren't showing xylene before and the xylene that's there isn't at a hazardous level. But *our* well, good ol' B-B-one-forty-six, already had a xylene content. Perhaps from prior dumping, but that's just speculation."

"This isn't all just speculation?" Adrian rubbed his eyes behind his glasses.

Shay shook her head. "We have data and corroborating evidence. So our well suddenly not only has xylene, it has *lots* of xylene. About twenty percent over hazardous. Then, three weeks and seven hauling jobs into this grid later, the xylene is back to less than what it was before. And all that soil has been moved way over here — wouldn't we love to have a soil sample from that area?"

Adrian waved his hand like an eager six-year-old. "I'll do it, I'll do it."

Shay pursed her lips. "You'll do no such thing without adult supervision, young man."

Harold punched the map in the vicinity of B-B-146. "I wish I could find out how much water was pumped out in that area, because the soil movement alone won't do it. It would take a lot of water, too, because the ground is mostly clay now."

Anthea set the ganache dish down on the table and began slicing. As she set the first piece in front of Harold, with caramel pecan sauce oozing from the center, he said, "I want to have your baby."

Anthea laughed. "Cappuccino coming right up."

Adrian was smiling. "Now I know the way to his heart forever."

"Chocolate is the universal aphrodisiac," Shay said. She eagerly took her first bite. When Anthea returned with the cappuccino, all three of them were thumping their feet on the floor and rocking back and forth in their chairs.

"Chocolate orgasm," Adrian said.

Anthea had the same reaction when she took her own first bite. She swelled up with pleasure and euphoria — it was either the chocolate or pride at having done a good job. It was hard to concentrate on Shay, who was answering Adrian's question about why the water pumping would be important.

"If we knew that they had flooded this area, we'd have them on two counts. First, it would be evidence of intent to hide an illegal act. That's one regulation that the EPA can fine for. Second, the illegal act is attempting to alter the constituents in an area already under EPA scrutiny. Not only is moving the soil illegal, so is pumping water into the area. But I don't think there's any way the four of us can get pumping logs." Everyone nodded in agreement. "So the logs might be mysteriously misplaced when the EPA seizes relevant records."

Harold whistled. "This is going to get serious, isn't it?"

"It's a serious thing that's been done. By diluting the xylene, they've spread it over a larger, unscrutinized area. Little by little, with every rainfall, the runoff into the bay is going to contain some xylene."

"What do we do now?"

"Well," Shay said. "I need to get into it with Scott about whether he's going to continue to insist the well sample I took — the one that started all this — is a lab error. Maybe he'll order a retest, but I don't think so. So I think I'll let him fire me when I refuse to write the report his way. Then I have cause of action on another front — wrongful termination."

"Isn't that a little extreme?" Anthea hated to think of Shay getting fired.

"My dad and I went through a couple of these kinds of things, usually called in after someone got fired because they wouldn't participate in a cover-up. The important thing with the EPA is to show intent to cover up. Fines are trebled and there's less chance of them being waived later. Even so, I could also get treble damages, which would hurt NOC-U a bit. I'd like to see them get heavy fines and take a stock beating so shareholders get angry, like they did at G.E. I've got no problem with companies making profits, as long as they do it ethically. And this just isn't right."

Anthea took a deep breath. "Seconds, anyone?"

All three plates were held out.

"A deadly combination," Adrian said. "Chocolate and anarchy."

"But it's not expensive. They're practically giving it away because they're upgrading the whole kitchen," Anthea said. She diced carrots and slid them gently into the bubbling broth.

"How did you learn about this stove?" Mrs. Giordano put a final pat on a mound of dough, then turned it into a large stainless steel bowl to rise.

"Well," Anthea hedged. "I was talking to a friend who runs a restaurant." Actually, she had called a friend of Lois's who had been receptive to the idea of ordering an industrial stove on Anthea's behalf. She didn't want to bruise the old lady's pride, but it would save her a great deal of labor to have six burners instead of four. And during the summer a heavier, insulated oven would keep the heat down. "It occurred to me you could use it."

Shay came in with Mrs. Kroeger on one arm, followed closely by Mrs. Stein.

Mrs. Giordano turned to Shay and said firmly, "This girl of yours is giving me a new stove. What will I do with the old one?"

Anthea knew Mrs. Giordano was hooked, but she didn't know about Shay. It wasn't as if she needed Shay's permission — Mrs. Giordano was as much her friend as Shay's after all these weekends of working side by side.

"Well," Shay said slowly, "there must be someone who needs a perfectly good stove, but doesn't need to run a mini-restaurant on it."

Mrs. Kroeger said she was sure Lily Wagner needed a new stove.

Anthea dished up fettucine noodles and smothered them with meat sauce. She remembered that Mrs. Kroeger liked extra cheese.

"But who will move it?" Mrs. Giordano looked as if she were afraid this detail stood between her and her salvation.

Anthea went back to chopping carrots. "I have these two male friends. I made them a ganache last night and basically, they owe me."

Shay was smiling. "Harold does drive a cute little mini-truck. Let's not tell him about the stairs until he gets here."

"The stove should be here, I mean they should have it available in a couple of weeks," Anthea said.

She started to blush as Mrs. Giordano gave her a sharp look. She'd have to dirty the thing up or Mrs. Giordano would never believe it was used.

Mrs. Giordano said to Shay, "This girl of yours. Are you going to make her an honest woman? What do they call it?"

Shay's mouth hung open.

Mrs. Stein croaked, "Domestic partners, that's what it is. A bit more of that sauce would be lovely, dear."

Anthea watched Shay slowly close her mouth. "I, uh, we hadn't talked about it. Yet. We don't even live together."

Mrs. Giordano waved a hand at Shay. "In my day this girl of yours would have been called a real homemaker, and that's no easy thing. Plus she works, she's smart, she has the pension plan —"

"Mrs. Giordano, please," Anthea protested. "I feel like a prize cow." And Shay looked like a reluctant farmer.

One of Mrs. Giordano's eloquent hand waves was directed at Anthea. "And she's got a heart of gold."

"I know that," Shay said, weakly. "I think she's quite nice."

"Nice!" Mrs. Giordano shrugged and turned to Mrs. Stein. "Nice, they call it these days. You should have heard what I heard this morning from downstairs. We never called it nice."

Anthea gasped and a carrot went rolling across the counter. Shay's face was gold-orange and the tips of her ears were brick red. Anthea suspected that her own face was magenta. They'd only stopped in to get some fresh clothes for Shay, and then, well, things had gotten a little urgent. They'd tried to be quiet.

"Don't tease, Sophie," Mrs. Kroeger said. "Though I must say I'd enjoy a wedding."

"That's it!" Anthea swept the rest of the chopped carrot into the soup stock and reduced the heat. "All done. Time to go." Shay held the door for her and closed it behind them.

Mrs. Giordano was saying, "At the rate those two are going, it'll be Christmas at least."

Anthea didn't quite know what to say when they went into Shay's apartment. For heaven's sake, they'd acted just like she and Shay were a courting couple, headed for matrimony, which was something they just couldn't have. "So that's what it feels like."

"What feels like?" Shay's voice sounded a little higher pitched than usual.

Anthea turned to her. "To be treated like everyone else. To not have to make excuses and feel limited and restricted just because of who you love. To have all the options open to you —"

"But they aren't," Shay said. "We can't get married."

Anthea drew her breath, pressing her lips together. She glanced away. "Why not? I mean, just hypothetically."

"Because we can't get a marriage license. Literally."

"But isn't it time, I mean, shouldn't we ... I've thought a lot about what you said about pushing the envelope. So what if the government doesn't recognize it. It wouldn't be any less real." It came to her like a thunderclap that she'd just realized what it felt like to want something she couldn't have because of stupid laws based on bigotry and fear. Thirty-six years old, she thought contemptuously, and you've just realized what it feels like to be oppressed. Welcome to the real world.

"Andy, it's not that I don't —"

"Churches do gay marriages now. And the government doesn't recognize that your family was wronged, but they were." Anthea felt as if all her nerves had risen to the surface of her skin. She felt naked and exposed and too vulnerable. Way too vulnerable.

After a short silence, Shay nodded. "My uncles would give their dying breath to have the wrong recognized, but that's looking at the past. I don't want to do that."

"I'm not talking about the past," Anthea said softly. "I'm talking about our future. A possible future." I've just realized what I want that I can't have because I'm gay, she wanted to say. *I want to have a relationship with you that no one can question or take away.* She had thought this was how Shay felt, too, but apparently not. Shay was being evasive.

"I guess it could happen." She smiled slightly. "Hypothetically."

She turned away to gather some books from the floor. "I don't suppose we could dash over to the library, could we?"

"Sure," Anthea said. Okay, they'd change the subject. It had gotten very warm in here, she decided. "Let me carry some." She was glad to have something to busy her hands so she could ignore the extra moisture in her eyes. Her emotions were jumping all over the place lately.

"You sure have Mrs. Giordano wrapped around your little finger," Shay continued. "How does it feel to be Our Lady of Largesse?"

Anthea stopped dead in her tracks. She couldn't have been more stunned than if Shay had slapped her. "Is that why you think I did it? Play the grand lady?" Her breath came in short gasps. "Noblesse oblige? Out of some . . . self-serving, philanthropic, do-gooder impulse?" She realized she was angry. Not just angry. Enraged. "Is that really what you think of me?"

"No, I . . . that's not what I meant," Shay said. "Maybe I'm envious. Maybe I wish I could have done something to help her so much. You don't have to be so touchy about it!"

"Touchy? Has it occurred to you that I might care? And that I might not appreciate you making out that just because it's easy for me to do it doesn't count?" That's what Lois had said. And that giving away money was all Anthea was good for.

"Count for what?" Shay stood with one hand on her hip.

"Toward my keep on this planet."

"I don't want to fight about it."

"Obviously you have something you want to say," Anthea said. "Or you wouldn't have started it with that nasty crack."

"I didn't mean it that way —"

"It sounded like you did —"

"You're being unreasonable —"

"*I'm* being unreasonable?" Anthea was so angry

238

she was shaking. She never let herself lose control like this. She hadn't with Lois, but then again Lois had said she didn't care enough to get angry. "I don't feel like going to the library," she said. She held out the armload of library books and let them fall with a resounding thud to the floor. "Call me when you can stand the sight of me *and* all my belongings."

"Andy, for Christ's sake —"

She stalked past Shay and out to the VW. She drove home sedately, then went through the house to the deck. She sat down on a bench and stared out at the shimmering vista. Shimmering, she realized, because her eyes were full of tears, and the tears were spilling over. She drew in a breath only to sob it out again, crying so hard she couldn't breathe.

Hot tears poured into her hands. She cried because she knew she'd been petty. She cried because no matter what, she'd never love her parents. The house had burnt down. Lois had cheated on her. She cried because her mother had been so out of it at her graduation that she'd forgotten Anthea had graduated at all. Then she cried because she hadn't put it all behind her no matter how hard she tried. And it still hurt. She cried because she didn't know if Shay didn't want to commit because of the money or because she didn't have any feelings for her beyond wanting to have sex.

The sex was great, but it wasn't enough. Not when Anthea felt the way she did. As if she'd just reclaimed her life only to find it full of Shay.

The flood abated somewhat — it had to. Her head throbbed and her shoulders were cramped, her face and hands were a mess. She went into the bath to wash and found herself crying because she wanted a cigarette. She looked at herself in the mirror. Her face was a mass of blotches and her nose shone like a cherry tomato.

The doorbell rang. She knew who it was, so she wiped her eyes and went to let Shay in.

Shay's face looked a lot like her own. Even though her nose was tiny, it was still red. And for some reason, it made Anthea smile around the edges. She sniffed and gazed at Shay.

Shay sniffed back, and her lips curved slightly in an echo of a smile.

They sniffed at each other for a few moments, then Shay wiped her nose on her sleeve.

Anthea finally managed to work a few words around the boulder in her throat. "I'm sorry I went off the deep end."

"I love you." Shay bit her lower lip and looked like a scared, bedraggled kitten.

Anthea shook her head, making sure she was hearing clearly. She was. She sniffed again. "I love you, too."

They sat down in the entryway with a box of Kleenex between them.

"I'm scared," Shay said. "I've never been in love before."

Anthea stopped short in the midst of blowing her nose. "Never?"

"Never. I've had my share of lovers, but both of us knew it was always temporary. It was easier than this."

"Do you feel like you're walking on a razor blade? The sharp edge?"

Shay was nodding. "I feel like if I make a wrong move —"

"I'll start being unreasonable —"

"No, that I'll hurt you. You've been hurt so much, I don't want to add to it."

Anthea felt tears leak down her cheeks. She hadn't cried since she was seven. Now she couldn't stop. "I just want to be able to give. Whatever, just give to you because I love you."

"You gotta learn to take more."

"So do you." Anthea wiped her eyes. "Any minute we're going to start talking about our inner child."

Shay laughed and took a fresh tissue. "I'll certainly stop taking your sweet nature for granted. I didn't know you had a temper."

"I don't let it out very often," Anthea said. "Usually only at other drivers."

"You know, I would have said my father raised me to know what I wanted and set out to get it. That's how I approach working. That's how I'm thinking about this thing with NOC-U. I want them to get nailed and I'll see that it happens. But, well, you're different."

"I'm glad I'm not a remediation project," Anthea said. She actually felt like laughing.

Shay looked at her with a genuine smile in her red-rimmed eyes. "You've been hanging around me too much. You're starting to pick up the lingo."

"You've let the genie out of the bottle," Anthea said.

"Do I get three wishes?"

"Anything," Anthea said.

"My first wish is to get up off this remarkably clean but very hard floor."

241

Anthea scrambled to her feet and pulled Shay up after her. She swayed as the blood left her head. Shay looked kind of shaky, too. "Next wish?"

"I wish we would kiss and make up."

"Easy enough," Anthea said. She took Shay's face between her hands and kissed her tenderly. Her fingertips felt the heat of Shay's skin as she brushed at the fringe of hair over her ears. She started to draw back, but Shay held her tight.

"My last wish," she whispered.

"Anything," Anthea said.

"I wish for three more wishes."

Anthea laughed. "Okay, but the first one has to be for another —"

Shay kissed her before she could finish.

"Is that your final decision?" Shay stood up so she could stare down at Scott. She felt about ten feet tall.

"The report's going in the way I write it. You're not here to decide our reporting policy." Scott sat back in his chair and tapped his pencil on the desk.

"Then I'll go to MacNamara over your head. And if he won't listen, I'll go to Billings. I'll go to Rosen if I have to." Rosen was the head of the project.

"And I'll remind you that your six-month probation isn't quite up, Sumoto. I don't like insubordination."

"I don't like false reporting," Shay said firmly. "I'll go to the Water Board."

"That's it," Scott said. "It's obvious that this employment relationship isn't working out, so I think it's best if we terminate it right now. I'll have a guard escort you off the premises. And only take what's yours from your desk. All files and diskettes stay here."

Shay stared at him for a long minute. Then she turned on her heel and marched out of his office before he saw her smile.

An uncomfortable guard watched her pack up her desk. A few feet behind him, Scott lingered, watching what she packed. Behind Scott the other occupants of their cubicle area watched with interest. Except Harold, who watched in glum acceptance. A couple of the other men had "I knew it was bound to happen" looks on their faces. Jerks, Shay thought. They'd never said a kind word to her. Shay gathered up her things and then gave Harold a grim smile.

"*Viva la guerre*," she said.

As she left their work area she heard a voice whisper just loud enough for her to hear, "How come the Chink got axed?"

In the blink of an eye, Harold whirled to face the direction of the voice and he looked *huge*. Several of the other men stepped backward.

"For your information," Shay said in a tight voice, "that's Nip, not Chink. The least you could do is get the insult right, asshole."

"There's no call for that kind of language," Scott said.

"It's a side effect of a hostile work environment," Shay said. He'd know all about that by the time she was through with him and NOC-U, she thought.

When she walked out of the trailer, her only regret was leaving Harold behind. He deserved better. She said nothing as the guard drove her to

Anthea's car in his little security truck. She'd kept Anthea's key this morning because they'd both known she was going to get fired. Anthea was going to meet her at the main gate when she got off work.

The guard followed her to the parking gate and watched her turn in her badge and trailer key.

When she drove through the gate she felt like a free woman. Stress poured out of her like sweat after a long run, and it felt wonderful. She had nearly two hours to kill until Anthea would get off work, so she took the Legend for a spin with the speakers cranked up to maximum.

When she saw Anthea, she cruised up to the gate. "Let's go celebrate. My treat. Anywhere you want."

Anthea settled in and said, "You know, I have this tickle in my throat. I think my glands are swollen."

Shay glanced over at her. "Oh, no, I hope it's not too serious."

"Oh, I don't think so," Anthea said. "Probably just until the weekend. Long enough to help you configure a computer and start working on your report."

"Oh, I get it. You don't have to do that."

"The old Anthea wouldn't have done it."

"I like the new Anthea," Shay said.

Anthea grinned. "Who'd have thought we'd be so happy for you to be unemployed?"

"Hey, I'm not unemployed. I still have my lucrative waitressing career."

"Sorry. I know," Anthea said.

"Getting fired makes me hungry. Where am I taking you to dinner?"

"I have a confession to make," Anthea said. "I don't know how to tell you this, but we've been together so much that I haven't been able to get my fix."

Shay gave Anthea a sidelong glance. What on earth was she talking about? "What fix?"

"I'd kill for a burger. From anywhere. Sometimes haute cuisine just doesn't cut the mustard."

Shay giggled. "I can live with that. And right in the pocketbook range for a part-time waitress."

Anthea walked two fingers across the top of Shay's hand as it rested on the gear shift knob. "I'll have to think of some way to thank you."

Shay exhaled with a smile. "I really, *really* like the new Anthea."

Anthea said, "I like her, too."

11
Freeway of Love

"Jesus Christ, Shay, this looks like something your dad did."

"What can I say?" Shay looked across Joan Lewis's cluttered desk and noticed that Joan had no better success keeping her salt-and-pepper hair in a ponytail now than she had four years ago. "He rubbed off on me."

"How did you get all this shit?"

"I'll never tell. Do you think you've got a case?"

"I'll have to read all the way through it, but I don't see where'd you'd make a mistake this big. Where there's smoke, you know."

"Does the agency have the resources to investigate something like this?" One of the problems with applying to the EPA for a job was the perpetual hiring freeze that was almost impossible to get around.

"Let me put it as delicately as possible," Joan said.

Shay braced herself.

"Ever since we got the fucking Republicans out of the fucking White House this is a fucking decent place to work. We haven't had a suicide since."

Joan hadn't changed a bit.

Joan plucked the pencil from behind her ear, saying, "Let me just skim through your summary. Ooooh. Tampering with a scrutinized area, I like it. That's five mil. Intent to cover up aforementioned tampering. We'll make that five mil times three. And the new administration isn't nearly as prone to waiving fines as the old administration. I think they're going to pay."

"Do you know a good EEO lawyer? I really don't want to go to one of the guys advertising on late night TV."

Joan smiled — it was positively feral. "I know just the woman for you." She scribbled a number down out of her Rolodex. "Tell her I sent you and it'll be her ovaries if she doesn't treat you right."

"Joan, my love, you're a good woman," Shay said.

"That's what's going to save the planet, m'dear.

I'll give you a call when I've digested your little opus here."

"I've got two numbers right now, though I'll be at this one most of the time," Shay said, as she handed Joan her numbers.

"What's her name? And is it serious?"

"Andy — Anthea. And it's not just serious, it's —"

"Fucking serious. Good for you, doll, good for you. The four of us will have to get together and do the fucking Michelob commercial thing."

"She's a gourmet cook and a little bit rich and I'm totally in love. Can't help myself." Shay realized that she would be proud to introduce Anthea to Joan. She realized she'd be proud to introduce Anthea as her mate to anyone.

"Why would you want to? Oh, run along, I'm late for a meeting," Joan said. She shooed Shay out of her office.

Anthea slid into the only empty chair in the conference room. "Sorry I'm late," she said to Martin. "I lost my car pool and haven't quite got the timing down." There were some sympathetic murmurs from other people in the room — the entire reporting and costing staff. She would have made an early start, but she'd forgotten it was the quarterly staff meeting.

Martin went back to his agenda. It included an announcement, to Anthea's delight, of the ability to hire some additional staff. She'd speak to Ruben this afternoon. The last item was a mention of how all analysts and department heads were to remember that they were not to talk to the press, particularly in this current public relations "challenge" about some toxic problem at the refinery that had been in the papers for the last three weeks.

Anthea looked nonchalantly over at Adrian. He was looking innocently in her direction. Anthea had been asking herself how she could go on working for NOC-U after what they had done. Maybe because "they" were a single executive who, inside scuttlebutt said, had acted in isolation. On the other hand, ever since the announcement of the EPA investigation, NOC-U had claimed the investigation was based on flimsy evidence from a disgruntled ex-employee, and was just another example of regulatory harassment. The ex-employee, a company representative said, was only looking for a way to bolster her civil suit for wrongful termination.

The company was doing everything Shay had said they would do. It made it hard for Anthea to find self-respect coming to work every day. And if Shay moved in with her and NOC-U found out, they'd know where some of Shay's information had come from. And if Shay moved in with her and she couldn't tell anyone except Adrian how happy she was it would bother her.

She didn't know what she was going to do. But she was realizing more and more that she might have to walk away from the job she'd said she couldn't give up.

Martin concluded the meeting and people began

milling around to chat before going back to work. Anthea gave a high-five to June Jamison, the head of reporting. June looked a bit like Lena Horne.

"It's a glad day for me," June said, her ready smile flashing.

"Me, too. I know just who I'm going to swipe from product accounting, too."

Adrian joined them. "If Ruben comes back he's going to find just about the same work he left on his desk."

Martin joined them and looked at Anthea. "So you're not car pooling with that militant anymore?" Anthea shook her head, not wanting to talk about Shay. "I'm surprised you could take it."

"I didn't mind."

June said to Martin, "Militant what?"

Martin rolled his eyes. "I wouldn't want to be accused of anything, but let's just say that Anthea's probably glad to not have some lesbian thinking God knows what about her every day."

Anthea was sure other conversations around the room halted, like in an E.F. Hutton commercial. She noticed that June glanced at one of the men on her staff, then at Adrian. As if from a great distance she heard herself say, "Just because someone's a lesbian doesn't mean they have designs on every woman they meet."

Martin actually laughed as if Anthea had made a great joke. "What are you, some sort of expert on what queers are like?"

"I don't like bigotry," she said.

"I'm not a bigot," Martin said. "I'd just prefer they didn't work for me."

Again, just about everyone glanced at Adrian, then at the man in June's group. Apparently, they thought they knew who all the gay people in the room were.

"Then I guess you'll have to fire me, because I'm a lesbian. And I don't like hearing bigotry where I work."

It took Anthea a moment to realize that the voice she'd heard was her own. She broke out into a sweat.

Adrian's voice came from behind her. "You'll have to fire me, too."

The other man everyone had been looking at said grimly, "Me, too."

June lifted one shoulder and fixed Martin with a look. It was the look of a woman who had raised four kids and didn't have time to spend on nonsense. "You may be my boss, but let me point out that this company has strict policies about the kind of thing you're saying. Andy doesn't like to hear it and neither do I."

Martin was turning bright red. "I had no idea," he said in a weak voice.

Anthea said quietly, "I shouldn't have to tell you I'm a lesbian to get you to stop making that kind of remark." A bead of sweat ran down the small of her back.

"I don't think I said anything all that bad."

"It was bad enough," Anthea said. "I don't like being accused of being out to sleep with every woman I meet. Nothing could be further from the truth."

"I didn't accuse you, I was talking about that woman I met in your car."

"It's the same thing. That's what you don't understand. Make a blanket generalization about her and you're making one about me."

Martin spluttered. "Well, I thought I was making a joke, but I won't say it again." He seemed to realize that everyone was listening. "I had no idea," he said to the group at large. Anthea wasn't convinced.

"Well, now you do," June said. "And it's a glad day for all of us."

"You'll never guess who I'm going to car pool with," Anthea said. "Well, for as long as I work there, but who knows how long that will be?"

Shay put down her satchel in the corner of the kitchen. She wanted a shower as she always did when she left the pizzeria. "Oh yeah? Who?"

"Well, these two guys we know. You know, the ones we fixed up? Adrian says they've been inseparable for three months, so they're getting an apartment together. They found a place in Montclair. Said they couldn't wait to have a view like mine."

"That was quick," Shay said. Compared to her and Anthea, at least.

"Adrian said they just click. Clicking on all cylinders. They had this long list of things they wanted to do and living in two places was slowing them down. Get this — Harold has convinced Adrian to try bungee jumping. Do you believe that?"

Shay nodded. "Yeah, I can see it. I mean, I can see Harold selling it. But I can't see Adrian jumping off a bridge."

"He said it was an intense male-bonding thing. Robert Bly, drums in the woods and all that."

Shay slid into a chair at the breakfast table. She was happy for Adrian and Harold. Mrs. Giordano was right. She and Anthea were taking forever to get anywhere. Anthea had only to say the word, any word. She'd been practically glowing since describing that scene with Martin. She'd been unpredictably sexual and bursting with energy. Another new Anthea. Shay loved her even more.

"That's not all the good news."

"There's more. Let me have it."

"Joan Lewis called. This is a direct quote." Anthea picked up a note and read from it. " 'Their balls are twisting in the wind. Tomorrow's news will be about a twenty-two-million dollar fine assessment. Tell her she's going to get a fucking subpoena for the hearing, but that may take a year to convene.' " Anthea looked over at Shay with a grin. "There's more. And I quote. 'The Washington brass is shitting bricks over the work she did and if she's looking for a job, she's got one. All garbage work, but it's a start.' "

"A job?" After turning over her report to Joan, Shay had felt decidedly let down. She'd increased her hours at the pizzeria again, kept an eye on want ads, and just plugged through each day and looked forward to coming home to Anthea.

"A job. A real job. One you could respect yourself for having."

"I'm . . . I don't believe it."

"She said to call her for the details, start whenever you want, but not more than four weeks from now because they have to close the position."

"I could start tomorrow," Shay said.

"Hey ... why not take a vacation for a week," Anthea said. "You've been working your butt off for months on end. We could go someplace ... drive up the coast in the Bug and stay at a B&B or something."

Shay felt as if someone had put a menu for life in front of her. She had her pick of one item from the work, love life and habitat categories. She'd gladly take an EPA job from the work menu. It looked like she was going to go on loving Anthea for a while yet. Maybe forever. And habitat ... living in two places was getting old. Especially when she'd rather live here.

"I have a better idea," she said slowly. "How about we spend a few days here ... maybe ... settling me in."

Anthea paled. "You mean permanently?"

Shay felt a rock land in the pit of her stomach. Had she been so wrong about Anthea's feelings? She nodded.

Anthea caught her breath. "I thought ... I was waiting these last few months, thinking you'd gotten used to us just going on ... kind of the way we are."

"I don't have to —"

"Yes, you do!" Anthea crossed the distance between them in a heartbeat. "It's driving me nuts having you half here and half there." She dropped to her knees next to Shay's chair and flung her arms around Shay. "I've been dying to ask you but you said to let you get settled."

The rock in Shay's stomach turned into butterflies. "I want to get settled," she said. "Here."

"I love you," Anthea said. She drew Shay's head down to hers, and kissed her tenderly on the mouth.

"I love you more than your house," Shay said. "Though I love your house."

"I love you more than Jodie Foster," Anthea said with a giggle.

"I love you more than pizza."

"That's not saying much. You hate pizza," Anthea said with a protesting kiss.

"I love you more than your cooking."

"I love you more than chocolate."

"Oh my," Shay said. She let Anthea pull her down onto the floor.

LOVE ON THE LINE by Laura DeHart Young. 240 pp. Kay leaves a younger woman behind to go on a mission to Alaska . . . will she regret it?   ISBN 1-59493-008-2 $12.95

UNDER THE SOUTHERN CROSS by Claire McNab. 200 pp. Lee, an American travel agent, goes down under and meets Australian Alex, and the sparks fly under the Southern Cross.   ISBN 1-59493-029-5 $12.95

SUGAR by Karin Kallmaker. 240 pp. Three women want sugar from Sugar, who can't make up her mind.   ISBN 1-59493-001-5 $12.95

FALL GUY by Claire McNab. 200 pp. 16th Detective Inspector Carol Ashton Mystery.
                                                                ISBN 1-59493-000-7 $12.95

ONE SUMMER NIGHT by Gerri Hill. 232 pp. Johanna swore to never fall in love again—but then she met the charming Kelly . . .   ISBN 1-59493-007-4 $12.95

TALK OF THE TOWN TOO by Saxon Bennett. 181 pp. Second in the series about wild and fun loving friends.   ISBN 1-931513-77-5 $12.95

LOVE SPEAKS HER NAME by Laura DeHart Young. 170 pp. Love and friendship, desire and intrigue, spark this exciting sequel to *Forever and the Night*.
                                                                ISBN 1-59493-002-3 $12.95

TO HAVE AND TO HOLD by Peggy J. Herring. 184 pp. By finally letting down her defenses, will Dorian be opening herself to a devastating betrayal?
                                                                ISBN 1-59493-005-8 $12.95

WILD THINGS by Karin Kallmaker. 228 pp. Dutiful daughter Faith has met the perfect man. There's just one problem: she's in love with his sister.   ISBN 1-931513-64-3 $12.95

SHARED WINDS by Kenna White. 216 pp. Can Emma rebuild more than just Lanny's marina?   ISBN 1-59493-006-6 $12.95

THE UNKNOWN MILE by Jaime Clevenger. 253 pp. Kelly's world is getting more and more complicated every moment.   ISBN 1-931513-57-0 $12.95

TREASURED PAST by Linda Hill. 189 pp. A shared passion for antiques leads to love.
                                                                ISBN 1-59493-003-1 $12.95

SIERRA CITY by Gerri Hill. 284 pp. Chris and Jesse cannot deny their growing attraction . . .   ISBN 1-931513-98-8 $12.95

ALL THE WRONG PLACES by Karin Kallmaker. 174 pp. Sex and the single girl—Brandy is looking for love and usually she finds it. Karin Kallmaker's first *After Dark* erotic novel.
                                                                ISBN 1-931513-76-7 $12.95

WHEN THE CORPSE LIES A Motor City Thriller by Therese Szymanski. 328 pp. Butch bad-girl Brett Higgins is used to waking up next to beautiful women she hardly knows. Problem is, this one's dead.   ISBN 1-931513-74-0 $12.95

GUARDED HEARTS by Hannah Rickard. 240 pp. Someone's reminding Alyssa about her secret past, and then she becomes the suspect in a series of burglaries.
                                                                ISBN 1-931513-99-6 $12.95

ONCE MORE WITH FEELING by Peggy J. Herring. 184 pp. Lighthearted, loving, romantic adventure.   ISBN 1-931513-60-0 $12.95

TANGLED AND DARK A Brenda Strange Mystery by Patty G. Henderson. 240 pp. When investigating a local death, Brenda finds two possible killers—one diagnosed with Multiple Personality Disorder.   ISBN 1-931513-75-9 $12.95

WHITE LACE AND PROMISES by Peggy J. Herring. 240 pp. Maxine and Betina realize sex may not be the most important thing in their lives.   ISBN 1-931513-73-2 $12.95

UNFORGETTABLE by Karin Kallmaker. 288 pp. Can Rett find love with the cheerleader who broke her heart so many years ago? ISBN 1-931513-63-5 $12.95

HIGHER GROUND by Saxon Bennett. 280 pp. A delightfully complex reflection of the successful, high society lives of a small group of women. ISBN 1-931513-69-4 $12.95

LAST CALL A Detective Franco Mystery by Baxter Clare. 240 pp. Frank overlooks all else to try to solve a cold case of two murdered children . . . ISBN 1-931513-70-8 $12.95

ONCE UPON A DYKE: NEW EXPLOITS OF FAIRY-TALE LESBIANS by Karin Kallmaker, Julia Watts, Barbara Johnson & Therese Szymanski. 320 pp. You've never read fairy tales like these before! From Bella After Dark. ISBN 1-931513-71-6 $14.95

FINEST KIND OF LOVE by Diana Tremain Braund. 224 pp. Can Molly and Carolyn stop clashing long enough to see beyond their differences? ISBN 1-931513-68-6 $12.95

DREAM LOVER by Lyn Denison. 188 pp. A soft, sensuous, romantic fantasy.
ISBN 1-931513-96-1 $12.95

NEVER SAY NEVER by Linda Hill. 224 pp. A classic love story . . . where rules aren't the only things broken. ISBN 1-931513-67-8 $12.95

PAINTED MOON by Karin Kallmaker. 214 pp. Stranded together in a snowbound cabin, Jackie and Leah's lives will never be the same. ISBN 1-931513-53-8 $12.95

WIZARD OF ISIS by Jean Stewart. 240 pp. Fifth in the exciting Isis series.
ISBN 1-931513-71-4 $12.95

WOMAN IN THE MIRROR by Jackie Calhoun. 216 pp. Josey learns to love again, while her niece is learning to love women for the first time. ISBN 1-931513-78-3 $12.95

SUBSTITUTE FOR LOVE by Karin Kallmaker. 200 pp. When Holly and Reyna meet the combination adds up to pure passion. But what about tomorrow? ISBN 1-931513-62-7 $12.95

GULF BREEZE by Gerri Hill. 288 pp. Could Carly really be the woman Pat has always been searching for? ISBN 1-931513-97-X $12.95

THE TOMSTOWN INCIDENT by Penny Hayes. 184 pp. Caught between two worlds, Eloise must make a decision that will change her life forever. ISBN 1-931513-56-2 $12.95

MAKING UP FOR LOST TIME by Karin Kallmaker. 240 pp. Discover delicious recipes for romance by the undisputed mistress. ISBN 1-931513-61-9 $12.95

THE WAY LIFE SHOULD BE by Diana Tremain Braund. 173 pp. With which woman will Jennifer find the true meaning of love? ISBN 1-931513-66-X $12.95

BACK TO BASICS: A BUTCH/FEMME ANTHOLOGY edited by Therese Szymanski—from Bella After Dark. 324 pp. ISBN 1-931513-35-X $14.95

SURVIVAL OF LOVE by Frankie J. Jones. 236 pp. What will Jody do when she falls in love with her best friend's daughter? ISBN 1-931513-55-4 $12.95

LESSONS IN MURDER by Claire McNab. 184 pp. 1st Detective Inspector Carol Ashton Mystery. ISBN 1-931513-65-1 $12.95

DEATH BY DEATH by Claire McNab. 167 pp. 5th Denise Cleever Thriller.
ISBN 1-931513-34-1 $12.95

CAUGHT IN THE NET by Jessica Thomas. 188 pp. A wickedly observant story of mystery, danger, and love in Provincetown. ISBN 1-931513-54-6 $12.95

DREAMS FOUND by Lyn Denison. Australian Riley embarks on a journey to meet her birth mother . . . and gains not just a family, but the love of her life. ISBN 1-931513-58-9 $12.95